SIMON'S CROSSING

SIMON'S CROSSING

A novel

Charles William Asher and
Dennis Patrick Slattery

iUniverse, Inc.
New York   Bloomington

Simon's Crossing
A novel

This is a work of fiction. All of the characters, names, incidents, organizations, and dialogue in this novel are either the products of the author's imagination or are used fictitiously.

iUniverse books may be ordered through booksellers or by contacting:

iUniverse
1663 Liberty Drive
Bloomington, IN 47403
www.iuniverse.com
1-800-Authors (1-800-288-4677)

ISBN: 978-1-4502-0249-7 (sc)
ISBN: 978-1-4502-0247-3 (dj)
ISBN: 978-1-4502-0248-0 (ebk)

Printed in the United States of America

iUniverse rev. date: 01/14/2010

Dedication

For Susan, beautifully strong, steady and loving, and my children David, Charles, Spencer, and Hadley Asher, sister Sue, brothers John, Steve, and "Big" Spencer.

In gratitude for Sandy, who has always allowed me to travel my path, and for my sons Matt and Steve, who always accepted their father's journeys as necessary.

For the students, staff, and faculty of Pacifica Graduate Institute.

The iU Editorial Department, especially Stephanie Higgins, Elizabeth Day, and Shellie Hurrle for their many fine suggestions and careful attention to the evolving text.

And for all others who have been, like Simon of Cyrene, compelled to carry their cross on the road of suffering and uncertainty.

Incipit

He was despised and rejected by others; a man of suffering and acquainted with infirmity; and as one from whom others hide their faces he was despised, and we held him of no account. Surely he has borne our infirmities and carried our diseases; yet we accounted him stricken, struck down by God, and afflicted. But he was wounded for our transgressions, crushed for our iniquities; upon him was the punishment that made us whole, and by his bruises we are healed.
                    —Isaiah 53:3–5 New Revised Standard Version

Let each of you look not to your own interests, but to the interests of others. Let the same mind be in you that was in Christ Jesus, who, though he was in the form of God, did not regard equality with God as something to be exploited, but emptied himself, taking the form of a slave, being born in human likeness. And being found in human form, he humbled himself and became obedient to the point of death—even death on a cross.
                    —Philippians 2:4–8 NRSV

Prologue

They compelled a passer-by, who was coming in from the country, to carry his cross; it was Simon of Cyrene, the father of Alexander and Rufus.

—Mark 15:21 NRSV

A life can be a river or a still pond. The river chose me. When? I'm not sure. I cannot measure in years the beginnings or endings of my life story any more than I can trace the origins of the stream that fed our well that morning when the Roman soldiers first appeared. However, I became this man, Simon of Cyrene, referred to in Mark's gospel, and I know I'm no longer the man I used to be. How could I be after the Roman soldiers returned that very same night, out of the deep darkness, to tear our lives apart forever?

The soldiers first came early in the morning. The sun at their backs, they cast long shadows before them. They rode hard down the road leading to our home, kicking dust toward my wife, Pricilla; my two sons, Alexander and Rufus; and myself. After drawing water from our well, each of us was carrying a small stone jar, and suddenly they were upon us. The four of them and the four of us. Horses panting, gasping for air, backing us up. Four Roman soldiers dismounted close to us, their eyes red and bleary, looking as if they hadn't slept. They stiffly climbed down from their horses as though unable to pry themselves loose from their mounts. At first, they hardly looked at us.

Then their leader spoke, too loud for being so close to us: "I'm Abenadar," he said to me, as though somehow I would know his name. Squinting his eyes, a long scar across his left eyebrow folded into the creases of his forehead. He waited as though deserving some acknowledgment. I nodded my head but didn't speak.

Speaking to me, he looked at Pricilla, who looked down and moved slightly behind me. Taking his time, he slowly looked around at us. He seemed to measure my eldest, Alexander, and my youngest, Rufus, carefully. Alexander locked eyes with him, while Rufus looked at me.

"I'm thirsty," Abenadar casually announced. "So are the horses," he added.

"You're welcome to drink," I replied.

"I know," he quickly replied. "You there," he said, nodding to Alexander, "bring me your jar. Draw water for these other two. The youngster, the pale one, Albus, who is well named, drinks last … with the horses." Then, turning sharply to Rufus, he said, "Don't just stand there. Help your brother. You don't want your beautiful mother helping me, do you?" He loudly inhaled through his nose while looking at my wife.

Pricilla moved closer to me. My sons both looked at me. Then Alexander straightened to his full height and suddenly said, "I'm not your …"

I interrupted him. "Son, do as he says. Rufus, you too. Get them a drink; water the horses." Alexander shrugged his shoulders, slowly moving toward the soldiers, while Rufus quickly brought water to Abenadar.

"More like it," said Abenadar as he shifted his hand off the handle of his sword. "A lot more like it. Your sons have learned something from their father, something they best not forget."

We were all silent as they drank, wiping their faces with the backs of their hands. Lastly, the horses and Albus drank. Unlike the others, Albus seemed out of place, hardly muscular, and his small beady eyes were set far apart on his forehead. His dark hair swept over his eyes as if to hide a wildly sinister look. He had barely begun to drink when Abenadar ordered them all to mount.

Abenadar nodded to me and took a final look at Pricilla, who did not look up. "Like my horse?" he said. "She's a beauty … and so is she," he added, nodding at Pricilla, seeming to lick the length of her supple body with his bloodshot eyes. Albus let out a strange laugh, while Abenadar wheeled his horse around and kicked it hard in the flanks, shouting at Albus as the four rode off.

I considered them a minor contingent of soldiers bloated with insignificant orders from Pilate, far in Jerusalem. I wondered what those orders might be. Like so many other marauding Roman soldiers, they were probably consumed with hatred for us so called "troublesome Jews." Pilate, known for his insensitive rule, regularly helped himself to temple money, and he flagrantly had the Roman emperor's image displayed on his soldier's banners. The Romans mocked our dietary rules, such as no pigs for the Jews. The Romans considered us lazy for not working on the Sabbath. Pilate's hot temper had infiltrated his leaders and the ranks of his soldiers. Pilate created fear and unrest amongst us and then sought to defend Rome against our protests. It was not unusual for just such a group to suddenly attack a small band of us Jews in Cyrene. It had happened all too often. We all knew about that.

The soldiers had so-called legitimate orders. They were to patrol for the next stirrings of a possible Messiah among us Jews, to be followed by direct reports to Pilate. Any recognition of a messianic leader among the people would supposedly stir us into an all-out revolution against the Roman hold on Jerusalem and its surrounding provinces.

"Think nothing of it," I said to Pricilla with more confidence than I felt. "It looks like they've been drinking all night. No wonder they're so thirsty."

Pricilla said nothing and walked hurriedly ahead of me. I looked at the slight swaying of her hips and simply tried to assure myself that of course they would see her subtle beauty. I thought these soldiers were on a small-time mission. They could, along the way, carry out their random pleasurable escapades and ride on toward some elusive glory for Rome. They wouldn't attack, not with my neighbors so near. And it wouldn't be just four against three. No, four against four. You couldn't count Pricilla out. Our neighbors would help.

Alexander and Rufus happened to be home with us. Wrong time. Wrong place. They had come from their own families in Jerusalem to travel with us back to the feast of Passover at our Cyrenean synagogue in Jerusalem. Their wives, Yiska and Nava, had stayed behind with their children. My sons had come by ship to Cyrene to take the long journey back by land with us. Together they had conspired to surprise us, to spend time with us before we all went to Jerusalem for the Passover feast. They would see us safely to Jerusalem, our most holy city.

Or so they thought.

I

"I don't like it, Father," Alexander said, watching the four of them ride away from where we stood, now closer to each other, watching them disappear in the distance. I reached up slightly to put my arm on his broad shoulders to reassure him. I could count on Alexander. He understood. He knew what was going on. It was not surprising that Pricilla said he was so much like me, while Rufus was close to his mother; he had even been reluctant to have ever gone to Jerusalem and left her here in Cyrene.

"Neither do I, son," I replied, hoping what he and I had seen, and Rufus had hardly noticed, would slip away as some unfounded fear. Pricilla, I knew, would say nothing, and yet she knew—knew all too well—that the Romans could hardly be trusted.

In our house, we soon forgot the soldiers, as the day passed pleasantly, absorbing the bitterness of the morning encounter at our well. Surprised and pleased that our sons would come so far to travel with us for Passover, we talked with them at every chance. How was Jerusalem? What about Pilate? How big is Justin? And our other grandchildren? How is business, Rufus? What do you like making the most—pottery or furniture? Alexander, are you really trading that much by sea with Cyrene? Why do you think the Romans are watching you? Selling much in the market? At this rate of questioning, the few weeks they intended to spend with us would pass quickly, and we'd soon join the caravan for Jerusalem.

On this first night of their arrival, Pricilla prepared a special meal, interrupted by tousling the heads of both her sons and affectionately stroking my, according to her, ragged beard. Her touch made the difference to us. Kidding her, we dodged her random grasping for us. Her warmth bound us together once again. The soldiers' intimidating presence became lost in laughter, the swirl of wine, freshly baked bread spread with fresh goat cheese ...

I looked at her for a moment, forgetting she was my wife, mother of our children. I saw the woman I had long desired. That hadn't changed. Her dark, deeply set eyes still drew me into her mysteries. I couldn't help but notice again the slightly uplifted tilt of her firm, rounded breasts, the tips of which had so often hardened at my slightest touch. She saw my look. I knew she understood, and it was as though she'd caught me with her knowing look. Blushing, she looked away, likely knowing that our sons did not notice the fiery glances between us, which would find us deeply into each other before long.

Later that night, our sons asleep and the two of us in our own room, she asked, "Simon, why did you look at me that way?"

"What way?" I innocently asked as I drew her toward me.

"Simon, the boys. We can't be loud."

"We won't be," I said, willing to make even the most irrational case for us not being heard by our sons. "Quiet, I'll be quiet." I knew she often rode our passion on increasingly loud moans.

"Simon," she said again. "Why did you look at me that way today?"

"Because I still want you like I always have," I replied.

Really, I had no answer. Her question curled into my rough hands as I deliberately, slowly rubbed the fragrant oil over Pricilla's shapely body, pausing here and there as a thickness in my throat absorbed any possible words. Her head tilted back, exposing her neck to my gentle kisses, which seemed to stretch her body taut in its need to find release.

"Not so loud, Simon," she reminded me as I listened to the ebb and flow of her increasingly loud moaning, for she had slowly and deliberately parted for my eager entry.

Digging her fingers into my shoulders, she cried out my name, as though I were far away, and then we both fell into a moment that I thought could last forever. I didn't know how much time had passed, whether it had been a few seconds or years, nor did I care.

And then her soft voice: "Oh, our sons, Simon. Do you think they heard?" she asked.

"No. We were very quiet," I lied.

"Sure, Simon," she said. "Do you think I'm deaf?"

And we laughed together into the final moments of release into each other. Exhausted, our bodies thrown casually around and over each other, silence enfolded us. Floating in some timeless place, only gradually did we withdraw from the moment that summarized the passionate intimacies of our life together, moments that had previously thrust Alexander and Rufus toward life.

Then sleep pulled us down and away.

II

They came just before dawn. There was no neighing of horses to warn me. I did not hear them enter our room and stand alongside us. I had no time to react. I flung my arm and body toward Pricilla to protect her and myself. Then came the blow to my head, and I was thrown back into the darkness of the night on the long scream of Pricilla crying out, "Simon, help! Simon, help me! Somebody help me!"

I do not know about the time that passed. I did not feel it go by, and I did not see the horrors of those moments. The time I knew began again with the splitting pain in the back of my head, pushing through my skull. I could hardly open my eyes. Tried and failed. Tried again. I tried to wake up. I saw the ray of sun coming through the window. I felt someone's arms around me. "Pricilla?" I asked. "Pricilla, is it you?" I pleaded. My head was being cradled. It wasn't Pricilla's arms. No, not at all. Not her arms. It was the arms of Rufus, holding me tightly to his heaving body as he sobbed uncontrollably.

"Rufus," I forced myself to say through my throbbing head. "Rufus. What happened? What's wrong?"

Suddenly, he shouted, "It's all wrong! It's all wrong!" Then I heard him blurt out the words that would last my lifetime. "Mother is dead. They took Alexander. I couldn't help them. I couldn't. I'm so sorry. I thought you were dead too. I couldn't do anything. They tied me up. Made me watch."

"Watch what?" I shouted at him in anger, sending a piercing pain through my head. I was unable to absorb what he had said to me. "Watch what, Rufus?"

4

"You know … what they did to her."

"No, Rufus, I don't know. I want to know. You tell me."

"They took her. First Abenadar, then the others. They forced the one called Albus on her. A soldier had to be able to do it, and Abenadar said Albus had his chance to show he was a man. He told Albus he couldn't do it. Then it happened."

"What?"

"Mother kept fighting back, fought each of them. She struggled the hardest against Albus. He kept doing it to her. Mother spit in his face. He licked her spit with his tongue. He then stuck his tongue in her mouth. She bit his tongue, tore a piece off, and spit it out. She fought back, screaming. The blood poured out of Albus's mouth. They laughed at Albus … laughed at him."

"Go on, son. Tell me. I need to know," I said, my voice lowering as something collapsed inside.

"And then he suddenly cut her throat," Rufus said. "He killed her. He killed her! They made me watch him kill her." Rufus suddenly screamed and then broke into violent sobbing.

I reached over and grabbed his arm as Rufus went on. "I couldn't do anything. I was tied up, Father. I'm so sorry. There was no one to help. They took Alexander right away. Tied him up. Took him outside. It was just me. I couldn't do anything." Rufus continued to sob, burying his head in his hands.

I got to my knees. I pulled Rufus toward me. I couldn't take in what he had said. My whole body was stunned, as if I had been struck again. I tried to stand. I couldn't. My legs shook so badly that I had to sit back down on the floor. I looked at Rufus in disbelief.

My wife dead. Alexander taken away. My wife dead, my son …

"Rufus," I blurted out. "I'm sorry. Sorry I yelled. I'm so sorry." And then I began to sob, my chest heaving with such grief that my whole body began to shake while Rufus grew quiet. I don't know how long he held me or I held him, but it was until silence took up residence between us.

Rufus covered his face in his hands and continued to sob, muttering how sorry he was, that he couldn't help, couldn't do anything, tears streaming down his young face. I gently pried his hands away.

"Rufus, look at me," I said. "Look at me." He slowly raised his head and looked at me. "It's not your fault, son," I said. "Not your fault. It will be okay, Rufus. Not now ... but it will." I could hardly believe what I was telling my son. "Do you understand?"

"I do. I do, Father," he replied with an equal lack of conviction.

After a long silence, I was the first to speak. "Rufus, was there anything else? Anything I need to know?"

"Nothing. I heard them talk when they took Alexander. Something about Pilate, about taking prisoners, a way to keep the crowds quiet. I don't know. I couldn't hear. They took Alexander, just took him away."

"I know, Rufus. I understand. No more for now. No more."

I closed my eyes. I fell into some place far away from what I had heard. I felt the cold stone floor press hard against my body, sending chills through me. My heart seemed to have fallen down into the stones. I couldn't get it back. I lay there as though waiting for Pricilla to come to me as she had in the past. I waited for the nightmare to pass. I waited for her to get up with me as she had done for so many years. I waited for her loving, soft yet firm hands to stroke my face, to part the hair on my head, stroke my beard, and say the nightmare was over. Where was she to shake me gently out of the night's terror? Where was the voice of my son Alexander? Her touch and his voice. Where had they gone?

Time passed as we wept continuously. We went to Pricilla, saw her lifeless, and could hardly look. I held her, and Rufus held me, and we were bloodied together. We covered her, covered the violence driven into her body, covered the agony on her face. We arranged her body the best we could, the way she would lie down naturally. I slept near her that night, tossing and turning, and thought she would speak to me again.

The next day, we carried her to the field behind the barn. We took turns digging, deeper, yet not too deep, not too far away. Our neighbor, his three sons, and his wife came and sat with us. His wife helped prepare her for burial. We gently placed her in her grave and gave her over to the earth.

Then everyone was gone. It was Rufus and myself. It had all happened so suddenly. Yet Rufus and I wept together, thinking of Pricilla off and on again, and then thinking of Alexander. Neither

Rufus nor I spoke of the awfulness he had seen. Did it matter how she died? She was gone now, gone forever. Any illusion that I was exempt from harm or encased in some magical protective place, and that I was the one to choose my challenges in life, died with Pricilla. Suddenly, I was afraid, afraid for myself and for both my sons. But Alexander could still be alive. I knew it. Rufus knew it. He waited for me to say something. Waited for me to tell him.

"Rufus," I said. "You've got to go to Jerusalem. You have to go now. See what you can find out about prisoners being held. There's no time to waste."

Rufus looked shocked. "I can't leave you, Father. I can't go now. You need me here, with you, with Mother."

"Listen, Rufus," I replied firmly, "we've got to find Alexander. Your mother would want that. He may still be alive. Find a caravan to travel with. Go home to your family. Tell Alexander's family what happened."

"But what about you?"

"I need to stay here a few days. I need to look in Cyrene for Alexander. If I don't find him, I'll come to Jerusalem as soon as I can. I'll help you find him."

I told him, barely believing it myself, that I would be okay. Sure, it would take time, time for both of us. They would want us to go on. We had to go on. "Rufus, you need to go home to Yiska, to your own family," I said even more firmly. "We've got to find Alexander. And I've got unfinished matters now in Jerusalem."

"I don't understand," said Rufus.

"There's no more to say, my son. You must go, go now."

"I know, Father. I will," he said, suddenly embracing me and sobbing deeply once again. I felt his smooth face against the rough stubble of my beard, and I feared I might lose him as well.

Then my son Rufus turned away from me, and a few hours later, he had gathered a few of his things. He stood ready to leave.

"We'll find Alexander," he said. "I know we will, Father."

"Yes, Rufus. We will. Do what you can. I'll be there soon."

Then he was gone, walking slowly down the windy road that leads to our home—and away from it—the same road upon which the nightmare arrived, the soldiers riding into our lives, killing my wife and tearing Alexander out of our lives.

And when Rufus walked out of sight, my own body seemed to fold into some place in me where I had never lived. I fell to my knees. I cursed the God who would allow this to happen. This God was absent. The humans he created and could no longer control were loose upon the world with their hatred and evil. And this God was powerless.

I hated God's weakness in the face of the sudden and random destruction of our lives. What sense did it make? What sense had it ever made? A terrible loneliness swept over me as I called down the road for my wife and my lost son. I did not see how I would go on.

Within a few days of Rufus leaving for Jerusalem, and as I prepared to leave myself, my despair began to turn to rage. Slowly, as though I stood in the midst of a fire, my anger began to consume my waking hours and restless nights. I don't know how it quite began. Maybe it was when Rufus left. I wanted him to go to his family. I also didn't want him to go. I wanted him to stay with me. Maybe it was when the cold stones on the floor of our modest shelter took root in my heart when I first awakened to her death. And Alexander was gone. Maybe it was my lying to Rufus that I would be all right. At some moment, in a time I still cannot name, I picked up my knife.

Each day, I tightened my fist around the knife. I began to want to stab … someone. No, I wanted to stab the soldier called Abenadar, the one with the deep scar across his bony left eyebrow. I wanted to stuff his scar into his eyes and blind him from ever imagining my wife again. I felt my hatred for the Roman soldiers. I hated their oppressive rule, even in Cyrene, their ugly temple to Apollo.

No, I might stab Pilate himself. I found myself thinking how I might get rid of this ruler, this inept governor who now ruled even the holy city of Jerusalem with an incompetent hand. Pilate's ruling hand resulted in these undisciplined idiots passing as soldiers, able to wander our countryside freely, doing what they liked, when they liked, and to whom they liked. Killers let loose on the land of our people.

Then I realized it wasn't Pilate, not even Abenadar. It was Albus. He had killed her. Sticking his tongue in my wife's mouth and then killing her. Yes, it was the one called Albus, the pale one. Speechless

Albus. Tongue-torn Albus. I would find him, cut the rest of his tongue out first. Then I'd cut away the last breath of his lust.

No doubt I would die. What did I have to live for? It was as though God had taken from me what made my life worthwhile. Yes, there was Rufus. But he had his own family. He would be okay in time. He would be able to find Alexander in Jerusalem. He knew people, had connections. He would understand what I had done. I would not wait around for God's revenge, which supposedly belonged to him alone. I would startle this sleeping God. I'd wake God to the pain of losing my son and my wife. I would not pass over my pain until I had the revenge my wife deserved.

I would die in order to feel Pricilla's touch. I would die in order to hear my son Alexander's voice. How else would I ever find them again?

III

I left for the Passover festival a little over a week after Rufus left to return to his family. Neighbors and friends had searched Cyrene and even the seaports. There was no sign of Alexander. No word about him. A slight hint came from a merchant who had been camping in a caravan about to leave for Jerusalem. My neighbor had asked questions about Alexander in the caravan, and the merchant said that a few soldiers had ridden by the caravan not far away. Not a soldier but a young man had his hands tied, riding a horse and mounted behind a soldier. That was enough to go on. It could be Alexander. No sense staying in Cyrene. Odds were that he had been taken away.

I immediately left for a gathering place outside Jerusalem, where caravans regularly assembled for the long, arduous, and sometimes dangerous journey to Jerusalem. I paid the leader of the caravan and joined them in the last moments before they were to depart.

Oh, I know my thoughts were confused at times, for my grief was mingling with a feeling of rage that I felt unable to contain. I took my knife, I told myself, for protection on my journey to Jerusalem. My heart was not in it, and sometimes I felt contempt for all the Jews who would travel with me to Jerusalem. Why celebrate some ancient deliverance? Who was going to deliver us from the evil that had destroyed my life and thrown my sons—and now Alexander's wife, Nava, and their children—into chaos and despair? I imagined I would shout at them that they were mere fools. They should turn around, go home, make the best of what they had, and expect no more from life.

My mind began to focus on a few simple details that would allow me to get close enough to Pilate. In the days before the caravan left, I became convinced that the only chance I had to kill Albus was to get close to the palace guard that protected Pilate. I had to get close to Pilate to have any chance at Albus, and I would be surprised to find that he was one of the guards at the Praetorium. Still, I would look for him there. Rufus might even know or be able to find out more about that.

The night before the caravan departed, a stranger who I had seen camped nearby approached me. I was immediately on guard. He seemed as if he didn't quite belong. His tattered, stained clothing and torn sandals betrayed how poor he was. Though suspicious of his motives, it turned out he just wanted to talk.

"So what's there to see in Jerusalem?" he began. "You don't look like someone just going for Passover."

"No, I am," I replied.

"Well, I'm not," he continued. "I go for the pleasure."

"Meaning what?" I asked.

"For one thing, I like to see the prisoner released by Pilate, his little show with the women and all. I like to see the woman the prisoner gets for a night, you know, one of Pilate's women."

"Don't know about that," I replied.

"You don't know much," he said.

"Maybe not. What's so amusing about a prisoner being released?"

"Not only does he not get nailed to a cross, but he also gets to have one of Pilate's own women. Pleasures for the night. She'll be right there in the crowd—not far from where Pilate releases the prisoner. He likes to hand the prisoner over to her, like an additional reward for escaping death, as if that wasn't enough. Mostly, I like to watch the parents see their daughter taken for a night. Then their daughter is set free. Funny to see how the parents react, especially the father."

"What's so amusing about that?" I asked. He laughed at me and wandered off with a twisted grin contorting his face.

Then it struck me. What if I could get close to that woman, the one Pilate would give to the prisoner? When Pilate entered the crowd, I'd be in position to attack him, or any of the palace guards, and perhaps I would see Albus, or even the one they called Abenadar. I was convinced I could do it. Maybe I couldn't escape afterward, but it hardly mattered.

Strangely enough, the more my plan came clear, the more I thought of Pricilla. The thought of killing Albus almost brought Pricilla to life for me. She would not just fade away in my memory. Already I could sense her presence—more alive than ever. And maybe Rufus could even get Alexander back.

In traveling to Jerusalem, I wanted most of all to see again the features of my wife in my son Rufus, his family, and the family of Alexander. I saw her especially in Rufus. Same brown eyes and determined look, a way of penetrating to what mattered, whether it was a sick goat on the farm or a frustrated member of the family. Together, she and Rufus would be determined to fix what had gone wrong. Maybe by staying close to Rufus, I could avoid the thoughts of her brutal killing. Where had Pricilla gone? Where was the young woman who had more than once fallen willingly down into a fresh furrow near the back of the barn, throwing back her long black hair while laughingly reaching down and playfully opening herself before me, sending me into a blurring desire for her?

I wanted to find Pricilla again in Rufus's even temper, which I had never been able to find in myself. I blew hot and cold, as Pricilla had reminded me more than once. How often she had said in an even, firm voice, "Simon, calm yourself." And listening to her voice, I did.

Both Rufus and Pricilla had a way, with few words, of bringing me back to myself, where my world did not seem to be painted in harsh contrasting colors. I admired Rufus's strong, muscular build, and when I walked with him, more than once I heard Pricilla comment on our sloping shoulders, as though we were carrying too much weight. Rufus would frequently throw back his head, a shock of hair falling over his left eye. He appeared to be briefly glancing at life and then retreating to consider it more carefully.

Pricilla often reminded Rufus and me of our common stubbornness, and now I believed and wanted to believe he would find Alexander. Pricilla once said we both knew how to place a dream where no one could quite reach.

We were unlike Alexander, who'd inherited the artistic talent of his mother and yet was quick to defy authority. He was always sensitive to the slightest change in my voice. How often my wife had to round off my own crudeness when I got angry over Alexander's sensitive nature, followed by a burst of anger.

Alexander loathed working in the barn. Even as a young child, he would easily daydream the day away, apparently thinking the long thoughts of youth, which were beyond the horizon of our everyday practical life. He would be the first to leave Cyrene for Jerusalem, and before long Rufus had gone to join him to begin his own work. How I wished I had understood better that Alexander knew more than I could see. He saw life more fully than I did. I thought best with my hands in the dirt. His hands were like his mother's, able to offer the precise, delicate touch during a difficult moment. I yearned to feel Pricilla's touch again as she soothed my life so easily, while at other times, she unleashed a seductive passion that swept me into her fleshy abandon.

Waiting for the caravan to leave, and rummaging through the few things I would take with me to Jerusalem, I looked at my own rough hands. I lacked Pricilla's delicate touch in Alexander's life. And now Alexander was gone. Regrets. Too late to tell him that I never really understood him. Abruptly, he'd been ripped out of our lives. I wondered if I would ever see him again. I could not change my past with him. Regrets would not contribute to my intentions in Jerusalem. I had to keep it simple, as simple as my hands. They were my hands, not Pricilla's. Revenge was not only to be God's. A powerless God had no such privilege. The task would be mine. I would find Albus. I would cut him open and watch the blood drain out, just as they had done to Pricilla.

I couldn't wait to get to Jerusalem.

IV

Around a hundred or so of us had gathered for a few days, preparing to depart. A nervous energy penetrated the crowd as people gathered relatives together, made quick runs into Cyrene for supplies, and formed small groups to travel together.

Then, like a snake suddenly uncoiling itself and heading for cover, the caravan began slithering toward Jerusalem. I found a place in the middle of the long line and toward the outside edge, where only a few people walked. Starting rather quickly, a jubilant cheer went up from the caravan, for the men, women, and children were finally leaving Cyrene for Jerusalem. Soon the initial enthusiasm subsided, and we settled into an easy pace that worked for most of us. Hobbling along, the elderly leaned on canes, carried a little on their backs, and brought up the rear of the caravan. Children ran back and forth through the line of us. A few young men, their wives, and children were in the lead. The initial excitement soon passed into an overall quiet, and before long the town of Cyrene began to fade in the distance. The long walk had begun. I moved mostly in silence, though my mind had already gone ahead to Jerusalem as I repeatedly rehearsed my plan in my mind.

The caravan consisted mostly of people like myself journeying to Jerusalem, as well as merchants; men and women with flocks of sheep and goats to sell in the city; camels stacked high with casks of wine, perfumes, dried fruits, and figs for the markets east of Africa. Occasionally, there were bursts of loud talk and laughter, and though constantly vigilant for marauding bands of robbers, there was a festive feeling in the caravan as we traveled.

I kept to myself most of the time, though occasionally I longed to be a part of some family. It was hard not to stare at a beautiful young woman who laughed with a young man giving her so much attention. She hardly looked my way. She didn't know what had happened to me. Why would she? If she did, wouldn't she spend the nights with me and wrap me in her arms, allowing me to shudder my grief into her body? But she didn't know. My grief would not be so easily taken away.

I felt a terrible loneliness as I plodded forward. No one knew the grief and anger that I seemed to drive into the ground with each step I took. Their lives were going on as if nothing had happened to me. Why wouldn't they? I was traveling along as though nothing had happened to them. What did we have to do with each other? Were we all just strangers traveling together toward some ancient festival?

Intruding was the thought of how Pricilla had so wanted to go to Jerusalem. I had been more content to have my sons visit us. It was their duty, I had told Pricilla. She didn't agree. More than once she had said, "Come on, Simon. Let's just go. Let's go see them for once." I had then withdrawn from her, made some excuses about the farm, the livestock. Why didn't I just go with her—just because she wanted to go? Was that so much to ask of myself? And then, knowing this, my sons had come to us. They would take us all to Jerusalem for the Passover feast. Pricilla and I could visit their families, and at least once, I would fulfill the commandment in Deuteronomy: "Three times a year all your males shall appear before the Lord your God at the place that he will choose: at the festival of unleavened bread, at the festival of weeks, and at the festival of booths." Now Pricilla would never go with me. Never.

My musings were suddenly interrupted. "Where are you from?" asked a stranger. He had joined the caravan some weeks out of Cyrene. A short man, he was taking quick steps as he tried to keep up. He wore a newer brightly colored robe, and his sandals were worn in comparison.

"I'm from outside of Cyrene," I replied.

"Your name?"

"Simon, just Simon," I said, slowing my pace so he could keep up.

"I've got things to sell in Jerusalem," he went on, as though talking to himself. "Business to do. Passover's a good time for business. What's your business?" he asked me without much interest.

"I have some things to settle," I said, not really wanting to continue the conversation.

"Settle?" he asked.

"Yes, settle," I said with more irritation than I intended.

"Young man," he said, "I don't know your business, but it sounds like you have trouble … or maybe you're looking to start it." For the first time, he looked at me, and his deeply lined face suddenly softened.

I didn't answer. He continued.

"If that's so, I hope you get to hear him first."

"Hear who?" I asked, not knowing whom he was talking about.

"The Nazarene. You know, Jesus from Nazareth. You've not even heard about him?" he asked.

"Can't say I have," I replied.

"You will," he said. "There's talk he's the Messiah … that he will overthrow the Romans. It's all talk. Rome is ready for anything. Same old rumors." With that, he slowed his pace. I quickened mine. We soon parted ways in the caravan as it continued along the dusty and busy road leading to Jerusalem.

At times, the days felt endless, the walking slow and boring as we wound our way toward the old city. People talked less and less. There were stories, however, of this man, Jesus of Nazareth, and his life among the people. Some said he sometimes even performed what seemed like miracles. They said the way he talked to people made them feel they could be healed no matter how hard their troubles.

These conversations drifted in and out of the caravan like a warm Mediterranean breeze. Meanwhile, city after city seemed to be passing us by even as we walked through them, camped on their outskirts, and went to their markets for supplies. I couldn't help but overhear the stories as they passed from one end of the caravan to the other. They annoyed me. Sure, I admit I was in no mood to hear them. At the same time, I found myself disturbed by what I heard. I felt a strange attraction to the outrageous claims of the stories about his healing powers.

However, I didn't like the way people talked about this Jesus. They seemed in awe of his words. Some of their talk sounded like so many fantastic legends strung together by naive people looking for some easy ways out of their troubles. Perhaps it was just the idle chatter of people who had become fatigued by the long journey ahead. This Jesus hardly struck me as a real person, and I thought most of the talk to be rumors and idle conversations among people bored with the long trek.

There were those in the caravan, especially some of the women, who seemed to think that this man called Jesus was willing to talk with them as much as us men. That didn't make much sense. However, when I thought about Pricilla, I wondered why she shouldn't be talked with like any other man. She had always expected that of me. One person even said Jesus was rather loose about rules on the Sabbath, putting people before the rules, and that had upset the religious leaders in Jerusalem. None of the talk made him sound as if he was about to overthrow Rome. That would have gotten my attention a lot more than these exaggerated stories of someone out of Nazareth willing to talk with women, lepers, and especially the poor. What was so great about that? There were always poor people around.

I heard one old man tell a younger one that Jesus seemed to carve question marks into what was taken for granted, was even expected, by good citizens. His questions and teachings often infuriated religious leaders as he shuffled his dusty feet into their pristine religious rules and observances. I myself concluded at the time that he lacked proper respect, especially for tradition. He also appeared naive about the powers of Rome. The man seemed like trouble wherever he went. Now he had sent troubling murmurings throughout the caravan.

I listened more closely to these stories than I intended to, and after a while, I began to feel even more irritated about this person called Jesus of Nazareth. He seemed just like the kind of person who made things more complicated. He talked of forgiveness and about what people intended in their hearts. That kind of talk made one soft concerning the simple laws of revenge. An eye for an eye made sense to me. I was tired of hearing about him. I tried to get to the fringes of the caravan. Walk and talk. Talk. It was all talk. What did it have to do with what I was going through?

One merchant told me that common people genuinely liked him because he told simple stories in a calm voice, modulated with some mystery, which mesmerized them while he befriended them. Common people. Who were they? What made them common? Was I a common person, educated yet turned farmer? And who couldn't tell a calm story if his wife hadn't been killed and his son ripped out of his life?

His stories, the merchant said, were friendly, and he was not unlike someone you would meet traveling and instantly like. His power, some claimed, rested in his tellings. The merchant said that you had to be still in your heart to concentrate so his words weren't lost. My heart was hardly still. The merchant appeared to have lost his bearings. I soon sought other company to walk with me.

The stories distracted me, though, from the revenge I found myself desiring with each step toward Jerusalem. Sometimes they gave me some momentary relief from the grief that soaked my anger into a smoldering fire that kept me going. At times, what I heard helped me pass the monotonous and long days of walking, listening to those in the caravan telling, for example, of his raising a child of a wealthy merchant from her sleep of death. Or another tale of driving the devil himself from a crazed man who was foaming, swearing, and kicking and fighting with anyone who came within arm's reach. The spirit of evil, taken from this man by Jesus, was driven into a small herd of swine, which ran over the edge of a precipice and self-destructed on the hard granite rocks below.

Evil! I could tell Jesus a few things about evil. Throw Abenadar and Albus into the swine and over the cliff. It was Rome that needed throwing over the cliff—Pilate, Herod, all of them. I laughed at myself and began to wonder if I was not becoming exhausted under the devil of the noonday sun. Evil cast into swine. Expensive for the swineherd but beneficial for the crazed soul who then calmed down and was said to have even followed Jesus when he journeyed to the next town.

At one point, I asked a priest who was traveling with us if he had heard of this Jesus of Nazareth. His response was immediate: "Sure I have. He has a following. But High Priest Caiaphas will put a stop to that. He won't let one man stir up the people. Caiaphas won't let anyone take away from us Jews what little favors we have from Rome."

"I don't understand," I said.

"What's not to understand?" he replied. "The high priest would rather sacrifice one man for the good of all of us. He's not going to let

Jesus or his followers get out of hand, especially during Passover." With that, he quickened his pace and joined another group of clerics.

After about twenty days into our journey, an elderly woman caught up with me and began to talk about Jesus as well.

"He loves the poor, you know," she began, catching her breath between steps."

"Why the poor?" I asked. "What is so special about them?"

She must have heard the edge in my voice, for she turned to look more closely at me before replying, "It's not that they're so special."

"What, then?" I asked.

"This Jesus knows they have so little, so little to lose."

"So what?" I asked, wishing she would go back to her own group.

"Their spirits are poor," she said. "They are close to poverty in about every aspect of their lives. Having nothing is never far away. It's easier for God to get through to these people. Jesus even said they were blessed."

She then hurried forward ahead of me and turned to face me, saying, "I don't know you, but you seem rich in anger … yet not poor enough to hear what Jesus has to say about God."

I lowered my head and pushed on past her. I tried to avoid her as much as possible, but as the days wore on, my irritation with her lessened. Angry? Of course! I intended to do something about it. It wouldn't be listening to some talk about the poor, although I admitted that he sounded like someone people gathered around with ease.

Once, another cleric walked with me. He simply said Jesus had no respect for the law, especially honoring the Sabbath. "I heard he healed someone on the Sabbath," he said, plainly annoyed.

It surprised me as well, but I said nothing. I began to think he had a different order for what was important. People before the Sabbath. Who had thought about it that way?

As I trudged along, I sometimes wondered how such innocent stories could get him and so many of his followers into so much trouble. Little did I know at the time how a few parables about another kingdom had already threatened some religious leaders, as well as Rome's hold on the country. Maybe he wasn't so innocent. A few of his stories seemed designed to crumble the foundations of the religious and political powers. He seemed to be going for those very things that held us together in our daily lives: a proper separation of men and women, keeping the poor and sick in their place so they would not disturb others, following the rules of purity and respect for the Sabbath ...

A rather mystic woman in the caravan said that he spoke from another place. She said rather dramatically, "He's bringing a new kingdom to Earth!"

Where was that realm? Sounded like nonsense to me. She was the one who seemed to speak from another place. I tried to put Jesus and these rumors out of my mind, at best tolerating the enthusiasm of those who wanted to tell me about him as we passed the time of day, usually when we were all simply tired and bored with the journey. The whole caravan seemed to have been salted by his stories.

I fought off any tendency to dull the edge of my memory of what had happened to Pricilla and Alexander. Jesus seemed annoyingly able to do just that, even through these handed-down rumors about him and his stories.

I had other matters to think about. What had Rufus found out about Alexander? Had he made it safely to Jerusalem? Could I really get close to Pilate and possibly the palace guard ... even Abenadar ... maybe Albus? I didn't like this talk of Jesus gnawing at my purposes.

Finally, not far ahead was the holy city of God, set on beautiful twin hills. The sight of Jerusalem in the distance caused us to quicken our pace, even though we were going uphill more as we approached the city. Hastily cobbled together homes with low-slung roofs lined the road. They were followed by dwellings built on top of each other and then the numerous shops that lined the road into Jerusalem. Throngs of people now crowded onto the road, thousands of pilgrims making their way into Jerusalem for the Passover feast.

Some, including the woman who had lectured me about the poor, began to leave the caravan, saying farewell to their companions. Some headed down side streets to join family and friends. The noise of merchants hawking their wares filled the air, as did the cocks crowing and the cattle lowing in the distant fields. There were occasional loud shrieks by shepherds with herds getting out of control. Some old women just sat along the road and watched.

Beggars became more frequent, and I tried not to look directly at them. Some were blind, and I looked at them knowing they couldn't see me. I wondered about the darkness that they saw more clearly than I ever would. Everywhere, the poor crowded the sides of the street, calling out for alms. The lepers gathered in small clusters, appearing to cry out for help from within a group, as though they were no longer made up of individuals. I hated to hear the word "help." Their cries reminded me of Pricilla's cry for my help, and I couldn't wait to pass them by. Who didn't need help?

The gates of the city were not far off. We pressed forward, proceeding toward Jerusalem, a caravan of people who had walked a long path together up the winding road, trying to make some sense of what lay ahead in our lives. We were dusty and visibly tired from the journey, yet there was a feeling of excitement about finally making it to Jerusalem.

Already this man's stories, this Jesus of Nazareth, had unexpectedly unsettled our journey. The stories that had clearly amused many of us on our long journey faded as we were swept up into something more sinister. Soon we passed under the shadows of the gates and entered the teeming city of Jerusalem. We were here at last.

When I paused to quench my thirst once inside the city gates, I heard the talk again. A political Messiah? No, a religious teacher. No, just a good man. A prophet? A deliverer? Another Moses? I tried to ignore the talk. The religious and political powers were clearly disturbed by his teachings. This was not a good time for a Jew to be stirring up the people. Too many Jews in Jerusalem. Too much could happen. Jesus had to be stopped, better sooner than later. The people had heard that he, the one they called Jesus, would be coming to Jerusalem. He wouldn't get very far, not far at all.

A blind beggar listening to the conversation simply asked, "But why? What has he done?" He said Jesus had stopped and talked to him, even though his disciples kept urging him out of the city. "What harm was in that? Why were people so upset about this Jesus from Nazareth?"

None of us offered an answer. Nor did we, or at least I, suspect the answer Jesus would finally give.

V

❁

Once inside the city gates, the caravan dissolved into the throngs of people preparing for the Passover celebration. I hurried toward Rufus's home, a vague sense of dread following me. What if he hadn't made it home? What if he knew nothing of Alexander? Maybe they wouldn't even be home.

No sooner had I approached the house than Yiska, the wife of Rufus, saw me and came running to me, sweeping me up into her arms and calling, "Rufus, Rufus, your father is here."

I held back my tears. I saw Rufus pause at the door and then rush to me. He threw his arms around me, and our tears flowed freely once again. Though unspoken, I suspected he too had feared we might not see each other again.

Yiska grabbed my hand and led me inside their modest home, which had an uneven floor inside the main door. Soon my grandchildren and Nava, the wife of Alexander, were wrapping their arms around me as well. My grandchildren, especially my oldest, Justin, kept jumping up and down, pulling on my robe. I quickly swept him up in my arms, and he buried his head in my shoulder and became silent.

When the room grew quiet, I turned to the wife of Alexander and put my arms around her. "I'm so sorry," I said to Nava. "They just took him."

"I know," she said. "Rufus explained. There's nothing you could have done. Yiska and Rufus are letting us stay here while Rufus tries to find Alexander. We think he's here in Jerusalem. We'll find him. I know." Tears welled up in her eyes, and I sensed she was speaking more bravely than she felt.

"Yes, Father, I do think he's here," said Rufus. "You know I have connections. Someone I know in the Roman guard told me that Pilate had many prisoners brought here for Passover. He has some agreement with each of the synagogues. If there's no trouble, he may release more prisoners for Passover."

"Do you know he's alive?" I quickly asked.

"Not for sure, Father. But he may well still be a prisoner."

"Why do you say more prisoners are to be set free? Why would Pilate release more than one prisoner for Passover?"

Nava responded in her usual calming voice. "At all costs, Pilate wants to keep the peace. He's brought prisoners here from different countries. He's told the rabbis in the synagogues that if they keep things quiet for Passover, he'll release prisoners that belong to their synagogues in Jerusalem."

"And?" I asked.

"So he may be one of the prisoners released if the Cyrenean synagogue and its people do not stir up trouble. That group, of course, is the most radical."

"Trouble is," interjected Rufus, "we don't know where he's held. We're not sure he made it here. I'm trying to find out."

"And of course," added Yiska in her husky voice, "Nava is right. The Cyrenean synagogue bothers the Romans the most."

Rufus seemed to see my hopes and fears intermingling, surely leaving me with a bewildered look on my face. I didn't know quite what to think. He could be alive. He could even be released. Held by the Romans? Where? And if the radicals rebelled at the Cyrenean synagogue, then what would they do to him?

"Father," Rufus said to me, "you must rest. Do not worry. I am searching for him. I will find him. We will bring him home to us. Our prayers will be answered."

I nodded, not knowing what to say, and soon the conversation went on to my journey, and how Rufus had made the long trek as well. I noticed that occasionally there were long pauses when I did not know what to say. I knew that at those moments, Pricilla would have spoken, and now my sentences hung awkwardly in the air; I found it hard to make small talk.

Pricilla had become the silent pause in our conversation—her absence so present. How quickly she would have engaged everyone. She'd have gotten down on the floor to play with the grandchildren. I felt strange. I was alone, no longer married. Rufus and Yiska were my family, but I felt like a child searching for a home once again.

For those first few moments, I felt strangely unsure of who I was. I continued to try to make conversation with Yiska. I talked about what was required for the Passover meal: unleavened cakes, wine, water, bitter herbs, and sacrificial lamb from the temple—to be roasted just before celebrating Passover. Yiska and Nava's friends and neighbors were busy preparing for the celebration. About a dozen of them would go to the temple for the sacrifice and then return with lamb for the meal at home.

A few hours later, as dusk began to fall, Rufus asked me to come to his shop. He was a craftsman by trade. He made jewelry, pottery, and leather goods, which he sold in the market each morning. I could see he wanted to be alone with me. I followed him to his shop. He pulled out a bench for me, and I sat down heavily, relieved to finally rest a bit.

For an instant, before he said anything, I almost blurted out my plan to get close to Pilate as a way of killing him or Albus—maybe Abenadar if I was lucky. I held back. I knew he would try to talk me out of it. Worse, he might try to help me. If he even knew about it, he might be implicated in it all, putting his family at risk. I said nothing. He slowly sat down and crossed his legs, leaning back against the wall. After a few moments, he poured us wine; as we sipped, we simply relished the silence.

When Rufus did speak, he used his usual few words. "Father," he said, "I am more hopeful than I said. I didn't want to get Nava's hopes up. I do think we can get to Alexander."

I leaned forward. "Rufus," I said, "What makes you so hopeful?"

"I cannot tell you much, but you know I have friends who are Romans. They have bought my goods. Some are even in high places. They heard some soldiers bragging about what they had done in Cyrene. He said one soldier was badly scarred on his face. A younger one could barely speak, as if something was wrong with his speech. He talked like a foreigner."

I could hardly contain myself. "Rufus, where are they?" I asked.

"My friend said they are part of the palace guard. They're in charge of prisoners to be released for Passover. You must say nothing to anyone, Father. My friend's life would be at risk."

"I understand, Rufus. You have done so well. You have given us hope. We will find a way to get to him."

"No, I will do it," Rufus firmly replied. "I have the connections. You must let me do this or the Romans might come for us all. Stay here with us. You'll be safe. I'll tell you what I know … what you can do. You must stay here with the family. We all need you now."

"I understand," I said, acknowledging the firmness in his voice.

"The family must be safe while I look for Alexander. As you know, Passover often stirs the people. Strange things happen sometimes. I'd stay off the streets," he added.

Rufus seemed to have become almost fatherly toward me. I admit I welcomed his concern at the moment. That the Romans possibly still held my son was good news. He might be alive. The small contingent of soldiers led by Abenadar and Albus, who had killed Pricilla, might well still have hold of him. If I could get close to Pilate, I might get to them.

Rufus changed the subject, although I barely heard him say, "By the way, Father, have you heard of the man called Jesus of Nazareth?"

"I have. I've not seen him or heard him, though," I admitted, grateful for a change in our conversation.

"The Sanhedrin ordered its special guards to arrest him. They took him to Pilate. He's being held there tonight. I hate to think what they're doing to him. For what? Tomorrow he will be put on trial. You know Pilate's usual Passover trial. Release one criminal to a young Jewess of Pilate's own previous lustful wanderings. Some trial, but the crowd will be there late in the morning."

"The usual place?" I asked.

"Yes, at the Praetorium, but I don't suggest you go there," he warned once again. "You know how the crowd gets."

I said nothing as part of my heart grasped the knife hidden in my cloak, while another part of me felt that I was saying my last words to my son. I hardly dared believe I could escape into the crowd, however chaotic the moment might be. Killing Pilate or a soldier would surely mean my death as well. I couldn't imagine what it might mean for Alexander. I had to be sure he would be safe.

I now knew I wouldn't go for Pilate first. First I would go for Albus, then Abenadar—if I could. Could I really dare believe they might be there as part of the guard around Pilate? So many guards had to be there. It was possible, though. I wanted that more than just about anything, and I did believe it could happen. While I couldn't risk the life of my son, I knew that no one would make the connection between Alexander and myself. His chances of release would be just as good. He would still be safe. Safe and then released, if all went well.

Rufus and I continued to talk about our respective journeys to Jerusalem. We even discussed the incessant stories about the man called Jesus, now to be put on trial before Pilate. I didn't argue with Rufus, even though he seemed drawn to the man's teachings. I said nothing of my plans and was grateful for the idle chatter. Revenge would be mine for the death of my wife, Pricilla. I had no intention of anyone interfering, including my family.

Rufus and I soon returned to the family, which was gathered around the common table. I then went to say good-night to my grandchildren. My eldest grandson, Justin, who had just turned seven, suddenly asked if he could see my knife, the one he said that I always carried with me. Reluctantly, I pulled my knife out, the knife I had not intended to touch until the next morning. I gave it to Justin handle first. He held it in his hands, turned it over, carefully touched the edge of the blade, and then made a few playful slashing moves in the air.

He smiled at me and handed me the knife. I suddenly put my arms around him, and held him much longer than surely either one of us expected. He said, "I want to play with it tomorrow." Then he turned over. I pulled his blanket up, under his arms just as I had seen Pricilla do. I sat watching him until he fell asleep. I watched him for Pricilla as well.

I left Justin feeling a strange uncertainty about myself, as though some resolve in me had been weakened by my grandson. I didn't like the feeling of weakness. I even felt irritated that Justin had asked to see the knife. I could have just told him no. For a few moments, he had dulled the edge of my anger, gotten in my way. I was in no mood to be distracted, especially by a seven-year-old, even if he was my grandson. I had to stand against those feelings, and I vowed that I would. For Justin as well. Someday he would understand. Someone would tell him what had happened and what his grandfather had done to make things right.

I did not think much about it as I said good-night to Rufus, Yiska, and then Alexander's family. Then a strange thought came to me. According to Rufus, I was to be their protector. But I began to wonder: from whom did they need to be kept safe? It was as though the answer was not my thought, as if it came from some other place. It startled me to think they needed to be protected from me. I didn't mean them harm. But would my actions bring them harm? Could they compromise the chance of freeing Alexander? I quickly put the thoughts out of my mind. I had a larger purpose and a specific intent. I would kill Albus for killing Pricilla. A life for a life. Simple and clear. My family would be just fine.

That's what I told myself.

VI

If the scripture somewhere states that God gives sleep to his beloved, then I must not have been his beloved. I tossed and turned in bed. I got up. I listened to the murmuring of voices below as Rufus, Yiska, and Nava talked. I looked around the room, where Pricilla had previously been with me. I paced back and forth, back and forth. When I did fall asleep, I was haunted by dreams. They appeared to sift through my hands like the grain I would casually hold, examining it before feeding my animals.

Dreams floated in and out of my awareness. In one of my dreams, Pricilla was calling to me. She was making love to me, willingly spreading wide. Then she was trying to take my knife away. I was fighting for it, fighting to have the knife so I could stab myself. In the dream, she was possessed by some strength I had never known—except during childbirth, when the fierceness of pushing out our sons infused her with an almost alien strength and determination. She grabbed the blade of the knife. She bled, but she wouldn't let go of it. She kept trying to pull the knife from me. I let go. I fell down at her knees, held her, and began to weep. I awakened for a few moments. Finally, I fell into a deep sleep that felt as if it lasted only minutes.

Just before dawn, a cock crowed in the distance. I got up as though startled into the day. I washed my face in cold water, trying to shake off the dreams of the night. Everyone else was still sleeping, and I was quiet, guarding my secret intentions for the day. I went over to where Justin was sleeping, and I took a long look at him stretched out on the mat on the floor, lying there so peaceful, so innocent, and so unaware of my presence. I almost kneeled to kiss him on the forehead, but couldn't. I was afraid I might just stay there. I might just give him my knife. How stupid!

I carefully closed the door behind me and stepped into the cool morning air in the streets of Jerusalem. The city had already begun to awaken. My dream seemed to follow me, and I tried to shrug it off. I wanted to leave it behind in the night where it belonged. What did it have to do with today?

I needed clarity, not feeling. Clarity like the sun, not cluttered by vague visions in the night. Would life ever be the same for me again? I was angry at how little I'd slept. I was angry about my dreams. I began to think that I didn't know how to live—except to be angry at the horror that had come my way. What else could I do? How could it be any other way? I didn't know another way.

Why would Pricilla try to take the knife from me in my dream? Yet why wouldn't she? Of course she would. But she was not here. It was me … alone. I was alone, without Alexander, without her. She would understand. Wouldn't she? Who was I trying to kill? Pilate? Albus? Or was I trying to kill myself? And to take my family with me? Why would I put them at risk over some incompetent Roman governor and a thoughtless young guy who was humiliated by Abenadar so he killed Pricilla? Who was the stupid one?

These thoughts followed me down the city streets as I headed toward the Praetorium. I stopped by the temple for what felt like hours, trying to make sense of the night before. What did Pricilla want from me? What would she say to me now? I wanted to kill something in me through someone out there named Albus—the pale-faced one. I wanted to do something to end it. *It?* I was no fool. I knew the "it" was the grief I could not stand anymore. Grief that had turned into anger like the soil I turned over repeatedly, year after year. My grief for Pricilla and Alexander, my anger for how unfair it all seemed, had begun to destroy something in me.

I arrived at the main temple in Jerusalem, which was already awake with throngs of pilgrims. I sat down to think, becoming more confused. Several hours passed. Suddenly, a wrinkled and gnarled money changer came over and sat next to me.

"Did you hear about him at the temple?" he asked.

"Who are you talking about?" I replied.

"That Jesus of Nazareth, who came here and threw over our tables. He said we were making the temple a den of thieves—that people need to pay for their sacrifices. I don't understand. Angry man! Nothing gentle about him. Scared us all."

"Not him again," I replied. "I've heard enough about him. At least he gets angry when he sees injustice."

The money changer gave me a puzzled look. I decided by late morning that I'd had enough talk. I'd simply take my anger to the Praetorium. Enough thinking about it all. This was a time to act, not think. I'd make my decision there, dreams or no dreams.

When I got there after a short walk, the Praetorium was already packed with a loud, unruly crowd. The massive stone building at the court of judgment already reflected the bright sun off its imposing structure, and the hard stones making up the square before the palace gave little comfort to weary legs and feet. The stones placed so carefully one upon the other seemed to defy any movement whatsoever. People were mingling with each other, talking loudly. At times, shouts arose from small groups, and gradually the crowd moved as a whole toward the elevated platform, where Pilate would appear, releasing the prisoner for Passover, a yearly spectacle many wanted to witness.

I moved closer into the crowd. Palace guards stood at attention around the main door where Pilate would appear. There must have been fifty or more. How would I find a scarred face in that group? I looked for the woman and her family—the woman Pilate would give the prisoner for a long night of pleasure. I didn't see her.

The closer I got, the more I realized I was in the midst of a chaotic mob scene. Never, in all the years that I have been traveling to towns for business and some relaxation, had I witnessed a mob of people stirred into such a frenzy over what seemed of little consequence. Releasing a prisoner happened each year. Why was this so different? Yet the crowd acted like a pack of wild drunks who had worked themselves into a frenzied madness. And over what? It wasn't what I had imagined would be taking place. I began to think it all might work to my advantage. The more distractions, the better.

I slipped closer to where Pilate would appear and mount the simple platform prepared for judging prisoners. My plans were not going the way I'd intended, but this could even be better. I had to find the woman. I had to get to the place where Pilate would come closest to the edge of the crowd. I would find a way.

VII

The crowd grew larger, the people clearly sensing that Pilate would soon appear with the prisoners. Shoved from side to side by the crowd, I fought to keep my balance. I was still too far from the raised platform from where Pilate would render his judgments, but the crowd began to push me closer, and sometimes I barely kept from falling. I struggled to get as close as I could. Suddenly, the crowd surged forward, and Pilate, surrounded closely by palace guards, stiffly mounted the platform, which was decorated with standards bearing the image of Caesar, fully displaying Pilate's disdain for us Jews who could never worship the emperor. One God was enough.

A collective murmur arose from the crowd as Pilate lifted his arm, passing it in front of him, the sleeve sweeping the crowd into silence. Some found that quite amusing. The silence lasted for only a moment. My heart sank. How could I get close enough to him for any of my plans to work? I couldn't take my eyes off Pilate. He mumbled instructions to his guards. Soon another ten to twenty of them formed another outer circle around him.

I scanned the circle of guards. I didn't see Abenadar or Albus. What was I thinking? That they would just appear before me and offer to let me kill them both? For a moment, I felt hopelessly absurd and ridiculous. My plan had no connection whatsoever with the actual situation unfolding before me.

Pilate's long white flowing robe was delicately embroidered with purple and gold. He nervously kept his cropped hair neatly in place by constantly running his hands through it, just above his ears, although it was cut so short that it was hardly possible for it to move out of place. The bright sun reflected off the round bald spot at the back of his head. I could clearly see it shine as he turned to give orders to the guards. His constant and rapid gesturing here and there to his guards seemed at odds with the massive stone building that rose behind him, housing a multitude of soldiers and government officials. His orders caused a few soldiers to leave and enter the Praetorium through the main door. At one point, his temper flared, and a guard visibly cringed as Pilate lashed him with his words.

Interrupting my fascination with Pilate, a small, fat man with a tiny head shouted into my ear, "Do you know the prisoner ... Jesus?"

I tried to ignore him. I was still looking at each of the guards, trying to see one of the four, but especially Abenadar or Albus. The stranger went on: "I've heard him speak, this Jesus of Nazareth. The common people love him. He doesn't quite talk like us. Ever hear him? He's one of the prisoners, you know."

"No," I yelled back. "I don't know. I haven't heard him. Leave me alone."

I tried to move away while keeping my eyes on Pilate and his guards. Visibly hurt, the man moved away. Spared from another story about this Nazarene, I kept my attention on Pilate. The crowd seemed to have grown to at least several hundred people, and I found it hard to move closer. Guards kept pushing the crowd back, taking short steps forward into the crowd and then retreating to an orderly line.

It was hard to breathe, and I sometimes felt trapped by the crowd itself. The air was uneasy, unsettled ... and unsettling me. Something was not right. The air had the ominous quality of a storm that is a day off to the west. The air smelled heavy, even a bit rank, and was growing more moist and sultry. Already I felt tired, out of sorts, and sticky from the heat. I looked more closely at the crowd, now beginning to search for the woman that the released prisoner would get for the night. She would be in the front of the crowd. Her parents would be with her. Perhaps a few guards would be there as well. Pilate would come close to her to give her to the prisoner in a sort of mock marriage for one night ... one long, pleasurable night. At least that's what I'd been told, though few people outside the inner circle of Pilate knew this would happen. I didn't see her, even though it was easy to see many attractive young women in the crowd. Here and there, these young women stood close to their families in small clusters. How would I ever spot that particular woman destined for the prisoner?

Not seeing the woman, and waiting for the prisoners to appear, I couldn't help but think about the many stories I had heard about Jesus. From time to time, I reached under my robe and gripped my knife, hidden for the moment I trusted would soon come. And yet Jesus and the reports about him were disturbing to me, and these thoughts came as unwelcome guests at a bad time.

I'd heard enough to begin to picture Jesus and his teachings. I didn't like it that an image of Jesus stopping for a beggar floated in and out of my awareness without invitation. What I didn't get was how this poor man—one who walked with no baggage or money; who went among the poor and the infirm; and who had gathered around him a number of men who had left their homes, their jobs, and their meager belongings to follow him—created such a fuss. I'd heard that none of those men were around now. But rumor had it that his second in command—the one they called Peter, but whose original name I shared, Simon—had denied knowing him, and then it was rumored that he had hidden himself away in one of the lofts in a house in the city.

While sitting at the temple this morning, I'd heard others say that Jesus had been arrested the night before. He had been taken before High Priest Caiaphas at the palace, where they were trying to figure out how to charge him. Now they had him before Pilate. Pilate would get rid of him once he knew that Jesus had claimed to be a king himself.

The crowd quieted down when there was a delay. Pilate could be seen talking to his wife. Some of the crowd sat down. I moved closer now, perhaps twenty or so feet away from the platform that stuck out over the crowd. I couldn't help but hear some conversations, though I was still scanning the crowd with hope that I would see Albus, or at least identify the prisoner's mock bride for the night. Not far away, a man and woman were talking. Appearing to be husband and wife, they were discussing what they knew.

The wife spoke rather loudly and close to her husband's face, her own face partly covered by a white shawl. "They took him before Caiaphas. Last night."

"What for?" the husband asked.

"My neighbor said they questioned Jesus all night. They finally charged him with sedition."

"Same old Rome," he replied. "Always fearful of us. I heard they even think there're weapons hidden around the city. Never found any."

"They beat him," she said. "He confused them with his answers. They made up charges. Caiaphas and some of the Pharisees brought Jesus here. I know they then planned to execute him quickly. They're afraid of his influence among the people and the synagogues."

Her husband simply nodded his head. "Jesus doesn't deserve this," he said. "It's all about fear. I heard Pilate is holding prisoners from each synagogue. He won't release them if there's any trouble. Rome won't ever let us alone."

Rufus had been right. Prisoners were being held. Rome wanted this nuisance of a man gotten rid of, and soon. Too many stories of this simple wanderer, a fine storyteller, having performed miracles that astonished and outraged many, had found their way among the people. He was to have raised people from the dead, both a young girl and a man called Lazarus. He was to have multiplied food to feed huge crowds who had heard him, changed water into wine, and even walked on water when fishing with those who had chosen to follow him. These tales and rumors got the attention of the Roman and religious authorities. Spreading too quickly, the stories had a way of eroding the proper attention of the people. Pilate, I suspected, knew that as well.

As I listened to the married couple, I began to feel angry again. Most of the crowd had gotten to its feet as Pilate stood. I now sensed that though a few people were there to support this Jesus of Nazareth, most of the crowd wanted to hear him condemned, even though it was hard to understand why so many had come to see his execution. The crowd appeared capable of falling into an uncontrollable rage. Perhaps Pilate sensed that, for he gathered more of the palace guard around him. In a strange way, I felt that Jesus was interfering with my plans, or was there a way he could help me fulfill them?

Yet what did this Jesus have to do with me … or with any one of us? I began to feel emptiness. I could just walk away from the crowd before it was too late for me, and even for my family. Yet my anger had me trapped. I had to kill one of them. If not Pilate, then Abenedar or Albus. I couldn't recognize the other two soldiers. These two I could for sure. A scarred face, left side. A tongue, half there. For certain, I had to kill Albus. If not today, then another day—yet preferably today.

I had to keep my mind clear about what I had decided to do. No distractions now. I had to find a way to avenge Pricilla—one way or another. Yes, Rome and the religious leaders had their Jesus. They had Jesus right where they wanted him, before a crowd swaying wildly with unbridled emotion. The Romans had killed Pricilla and imprisoned my son. I would now bring horror to them as well, at least a few of them, especially the one named Albus, the one missing part of his tongue—thanks to Pricilla. Thanks to me, Albus would soon lose the rest of his tongue forever.

I needed to be patient. I'd wait for the right moment. It was not far away.

VIII

The crowd suddenly surged forward as the prisoners were brought before Pilate. People were shoving and jostling each other as they struggled to get closer to the platform that jutted out toward them, elevating Pilate above the crowd. I managed to get close enough to see both prisoners.

I recognized the prisoner closest to Pilate. He was the one called Jesus. He was the one so many had talked about and described, except he was horribly beaten. The other prisoner raised his fist and shook it toward the crowd. A guard struck him on the back.

"It's Barabbas!" a woman in the crowd shrieked, and there was laughter in the crowd. "He's a killer," she said. The guards were keeping Barabbas, a husky defiant-looking man, in the background.

I was now close enough that if Pilate went directly down from the platform to the crowd, he would have to pass close to me. He would give his chosen woman to the released prisoner. I would be close enough to him and to his guards to strike at one of them. Perhaps only a few guards would come with him. Maybe Abenadar. Maybe Albus, partial-tongue Albus. I had to find Pilate's woman, though. Only two or three in the front of the crowd seemed likely candidates. I eyed a young woman in particular. She had long dark hair thrown to one side of her head, and a man and a woman who looked like her parents were close by her side. She was looking down at the ground, and her father was partly holding her up. I wasn't sure if she was the woman I'd been seeking, though, and I found myself moving closer to her. As I did, I saw the beauty of her eyes and the partially hidden and partly revealed curves of her body.

I felt for my knife again, assuring myself that it was still in place.

The crowd's focus was now on Jesus. He had suffered a severe beating, his face so swollen that it swallowed the features of his face, his hair torn in places, his head fallen down and forward ... He was clearly exhausted and in excruciating pain.

Seeing him, I took a step backward. Suddenly, I also saw Pricilla calling out to me for help, with me unable to prevent her cruel and merciless death. I also felt the terrible emptiness of my son Alexander missing from my life. He seemed to have disappeared forever. How would I find him? I felt an unexpected helplessness in me as I stared, along with the crowd, at the prisoner who was barely able to stand before Pilate. He would not look directly at Jesus as he kept surveying the crowd, now packed closely together, not far from him. The guards had tightened the two-deep circle around him, and some had even begun to surround the crowd.

Yet it all blurred before me in that moment. When I recovered a bit, I noticed the robe Jesus was wearing. Torn right down the front, it exposed the deep red welts lashed across his body. This man a threat to the regime? How stupid to think so.

Was Jesus even worth executing? Somehow, looking at Jesus, my hatred for Pilate and Rome itself felt, even to me, a bit strange. For an instant, I thought I had stepped into a story that made no sense. Looking at Jesus and back at myself, I felt out of place. What was I doing here in the crowd? I started to feel childish, as though carrying all that anger and hatred was just as foolish as all this anger and hatred directed toward Jesus. Only by placing my hand quickly on my knife did I began to come back to my senses, or so I thought.

Meanwhile, the crowd grew louder as it jeered at the prisoners, offering their own threats. Many seemed to have been up drinking heavily the night before, and I could smell the wine on their breath. A man next to me suddenly vomited onto the sandals of a young boy, and the father of the boy swung wildly at the lurching drunkard. The crowd appeared aimless, seeking any distraction, searching for someone or something upon which to release its restlessness and brutal behavior. Occasionally, a loud howl arose from the crowd, and like a pack of rabid animals, others in the crowd answered the howl. It was hard to understand what was happening. It was as though each person had brought to the moment his darkest side, and now they were all joining together to target the prisoner named Jesus.

Looking at Jesus standing before Pilate, I couldn't help but wonder if I was not as ridiculous as the rest of the crowd. Was I one of them as well? No, I told myself, I was different. I had a purpose for being there. The individuals in the crowd had no purpose other than the release of their hatred and anger on some unknown, and by all accounts, innocent man. There was blood in their eyes, blood marinated in frustration with Rome, and hatred for being ruled by a foreign country. They were not going to be satisfied until they saw blood on this rebel. The people in the crowd seemed to be searching for some way to quell their restless anger. Sacrificing their Passover lambs at the temple was not enough. I had no quarrel with Jesus, none whatsoever. He was barely a rumor to me, although now that I saw him, I could hardly look away. How could this have happened to this man called Jesus for seemingly no reason at all? I didn't know what to make of it.

Jesus was a marked sacrifice. As I watched him, I noted that he was apparently offering no resistance, and unlike Barabbas, there seemed to be no defiance of the powers that now sought to execute him. He was not resigned, yet he was not resistant. He was clearly accepting of what was happening to him, and only on occasion did he raise his head and look toward us in the crowd. When he did, a silence descended on most of the crowd for a few moments. He hardly appeared to be a violent person, and yet the crowd appeared to resent his quiet demeanor.

A strange feeling of helplessness began to suffocate me. Jesus could do nothing. Neither could I. I couldn't for Pricilla. I wasn't sure I could help Alexander. I couldn't even help myself, and I wished for a moment that I could do something for this helpless man who was suffering so horribly. And for what? And why was I suffering? What had I done to lose my son? To have my wife killed? It was getting hard to breathe.

Jesus was calm and appeared submissive in his torn garments. It was as though he had just accepted the beating he had received the night before. Didn't he fight back? Why did they not simply execute him under the cover of night? What did they hope to gain by this early morning charade, among a crowd ready to explode, so ignited were they with rage? If they were to fear anyone, it should be this crowd, not the beaten pulp of a man now standing serenely in front of them.

"Let him go," I found myself muttering under my breath. "Please, for God's sake, let this man go." When I said this to myself, I recognized the pain welling up in me, making me want to cry out to someone to let my own suffering go. I could hardly stand the grief and anger that had whipped and scourged my own life with such sudden violence.

A younger man next to me asked his friend, "Who is he? What are they holding him for?"

"He wants to take over the Roman legion," his older companion responded.

"But he is pitiful in appearance. What could he do to upset the authorities?" the younger asked.

"They say he's some sort of healer," replied his elder. "He seems to speak directly to God, and some claim he's like God come down to Earth, and yet born to be like us."

I interrupted them both and asked, "Is that what he says, or is that what others say about him?"

They could give no answer, though the elder asked, "What's the difference to Rome? Any threat to their power is excuse enough to get rid of him."

I strained to see Jesus more clearly. Some Roman soldier had fashioned a twisted wreath of thorns together and placed it on Jesus's head. To complete the mockery, one of them had fashioned a reed to resemble a scepter and placed it in his right hand.

Why such humility in this man? I was annoyed that it bothered me so much, interfering with my own purposes. I'm not sure what bothered me so much. Perhaps it was because I resented my own weakness, and I therefore couldn't stand to see it in him. Yet was it weakness that I was seeing? I wondered why I had not been able to fight off the soldiers and help Pricilla. I despised Albus, who couldn't stand up to Abenadar, and in a show of false courage, had killed Pricilla. Maybe that was it. Here was another weak man, a victim of Rome. Hardly a Messiah. What a laugh that was.

Then again, perhaps I just couldn't stand the sight of what was happening before me. Jesus held a scepter, a silly green reed swaying in the wind. I would soon hold my knife. The scepter was pure mockery of his alleged kingdom that was not of this world. My knife was real. Hard, cold steel forged by me while my grandson Justin watched, and when I finished my work, I put his tiny hand upon it as well. Could I give my knife to Jesus and take the scepter instead? What a strange thought, and where was it coming from? I hated the thought. I despised my own weakness and the weaknesses of others, and I would not surrender to my helplessness ever again.

Jesus was another helpless victim of the power of Rome, and Rome intended to make a spectacle of his weakness. This public outrage was quickly unfolding before me. A man who, only two days before, in the narrow back streets of Jerusalem, was telling stories quietly to anyone who was interested was being publicly destroyed.

What a celebration, I learned, had occurred when he'd entered the city with his band of devoted men and women. He was greeted as a hero who would have the power to take on Rome. It wasn't clear how. Other potential messiahs had always failed. How did things turn so brutish in such a short time? What was at work here? And where were his followers now that he needed support? He hardly had an army with weapons of even minimal destruction hidden about the city. Were his followers hidden somewhere in this crowd, waiting for the right moment to suddenly attack the Romans?

I had no answers to any of these questions, and I even wondered why I was giving it all so much attention. I felt as if I had been drawn into an unfolding story that I did not intend to continue witnessing. I had to stay focused on what I intended to do as soon as the opportunity presented itself. I couldn't get distracted now. Then the helplessness I felt for Jesus unexpectedly broke again into the sense of utter helplessness I had experienced at Pricilla's death. Anger began to well up in me once more. I wanted to do something—like take this crowd down and beat it into the earth. Yet I could hardly move to avoid being trampled. The crowd had a mysterious animal energy that fascinated and frightened me. Now it seemed to close in on me, and it was as though the people close to me were pushing their anger into me as they focused on the prisoners before Pilate. At times, I felt so trapped by those immediately around me that I wondered how I could ever move fast enough to strike with my knife, even if I had the chance.

Several guards brought Jesus closer to the steps of the platform, which they had erected in front of the main door leading out of the Praetorium. His shoulders slumped even more than when I had first seen him. He leaned down and forward as though being pulled toward the earth. His head was now bleeding heavily from the crown of thorns that had been pressed hard into his skull so it would not slip off while he was interrogated publicly. Moving slowly, feet bare, shuffling rather than walking, Jesus made his way before Pilate. He was almost naked as he stood in front of the helmeted and armored Roman soldiers and the regal uniforms of Imperial Rome. I thought it such a pitiful contrast. He stood like David before a group of Goliaths swarming him like so many giant gnats. Jesus was now only thirty or forty feet from me, and those of us in the crowd close to him followed his every move. I could see from the separate puncture wounds on his head, inflicted by the thorns, that he had already lost much blood from this crown. He had deep, nasty gashes across his arms and chest. It made me think he would not last through the interrogation.

I could see Jesus's face, exhausted but not defeated. He hardly spoke, and I could barely make out his words. He was offering no defense in either word or act. He simply stood there.

By the crowd's response to his plight, you could tell he was hurt. While he looked at us, it seemed no one was looking at him, only at the outward movements of his body. In response to the crowd's anger, he would suddenly hang his head as though feeling helpless before their vehement condemnations. I sometimes saw him look directly at the crowd, seeming to pick out a few individuals to focus on. Once he glanced my way, but I think he was really looking at a young child not far from where I stood. The child seemed transfixed by seeing him so wounded. The crowd looked with one eye upon him, or so it appeared to me. I do not know what the crowd saw, but I'm sure the people did not see him at all. He was now the object of their irrational hatred.

I looked around at the faces of the crowd nearest to me. Why the anger on the mother's face? The scowl of the old man? The laughter of a young boy with his friends? The jeering of a young child? Why the waves of anger? Was it fear? Did they feel safe surrounded by Roman guards, enough of them to yell without being held accountable? Were they not part of Pilate's public show, filling their roles perfectly?

Why were these people so frightened? I wondered if they thought they could kill their fear by killing this Jesus from Nazareth. Did they really believe he had the capacity or the followers to carry out an effective insurrection? Maybe they were disappointed that he couldn't. Was he such a threat to Rome or, for that matter, to our Jewish thought and practice? How absurd it all seemed.

However, I felt it myself, the raging hatred trying to find a place to unleash its fury. Was I so different from this crowd? Among the entire crowd, was I not the one who sought to kill Pilate's inept, brutal guards if given the chance? Wasn't my hatred of Rome justified? Who could blame me for my desire to take out Pilate, Abenadar, or Albus if they knew my story?

Yet I could barely stand to watch what was happening. Suddenly, my own anguish diminished in relation to what was taking place before me. I could hardly see Pilate because of the growing throng, although I caught glimpses of him pacing back and forth while speaking. He punctuated this by intermittently slumping into the elegant chair that had been a gift to him from my own place of birth, Cyrene, the capital city of the North African district of Cyrenaica. That chair had been just one among many attempts to buy some favor and assurances that his often harsh arbitrary judgments would not fall on our city.

Now it seemed that Pilate was entertaining himself and the crowd with his questioning of Jesus.

"Who do you say you are? Have you nothing to say? Where are you from? Do you think you're some kind of God? What other kingdom are you talking about? Have you nothing to say for yourself?"

It was obvious that Pilate wanted to appear clever and powerful in his interrogation. Yet his questions had no answers, except the distant sound of nails that would soon be driven through Jesus's flesh and into a wooden beam neatly placed along one wall of the courtyard. Pilate had already begun to crucify Jesus. The crowd was pleased, and some of the people chanted back Pilate's questions. Once in a while, Jesus looked at us with a puzzled and painful look that caused many to grow silent.

The crowd kept growing, and growing louder, as Pilate's overbearing presence drew the attention of the rabble, which was on the brink of frenzy. The fragmented crowd began to shape itself into a unified vision, with every eye scanning the scene above and in front of us. We could hear him even above the din that rose and fell with his words.

Pilate appeared full of authority in his purple, blue, and red uniform and his regal bearing. He seemed a man who was untouchable and possessing absolute power. Yet as he spoke, his stature appeared to shrink before us. His words were so small for his dress. He had little persuasive effect. He appeared cowardly and small-minded, something the stinking, angry, and frothy crowd seemed to quickly sense. In fact, he was not much different from the Roman-appointed governor of Cyrenaica at home. But Pilate, to his credit, looked more the part. I heard him above the din of the crowd, clearly uneasy with his morning's task, say to Jesus, in what was more a question directed at the crowd's ears, "Are you the king of the Jews who claims to be the son of God?"

The crowd's shouts suddenly ceased, and it seemed to even suck in a collective breath for an instant as the prisoner answered, "It is you who say that I am," he replied.

It was as if his words unlocked all the anger and rage the people had pent up in them from Rome's oppression. Now they went wild, a kind of ecstatic and yet menacing rage that threatened to tear down the pillars of the palace with their noise. There was no way out for this Nazarene, surrounded as he was by the impersonal rancor of the crowd.

Pilate was glancing across the heads of the crowd and seemingly realizing with a sudden shock that he really had no control over such chaos forming in front of him. "Move this charade along!" I heard him shout to his lieutenants. "The crowd wants blood. Let it not be ours."

Pilate then quieted the crowd with a question. The crowd listened intently. "Where do you come from?" Pilate inquired in a futile effort to be clever. Perhaps he did not know what he was asking. I thought this a strange question, and from what others said, I wasn't alone.

"Does he mean what district is he from?" one old woman asked.

"No, I think he is asking where he was born," offered a man about my age.

But I had another feeling about this strange question. I believe Pilate was using this opportunity to ask Jesus who he was, what manner of person he was, and what was the mystery of his power. There was something pathetic in the way he asked the question. He almost seemed genuine ... but not enough to show weakness. I wondered if he somehow sensed that if he knew who this man was, he might know more who he was. When the defeated man met Pilate's inquiries with silence, those of us close enough to the front of the crowd could hear the governor tell Jesus that he had the power to release him. Together they needed to find a way to appease the crowd and disarm the tension in the charged plaza.

The crowd grew quiet waiting for Jesus's response. He answered Pilate, "You would have no power over me if it had not been given you from above."

"No one gives me my power," Pilate snapped back, while at the same time looking bewildered by Jesus's response. Next, I heard him mutter aloud to those around him, "Who cursed me with this command?" Pilate addressed no one in particular as he surveyed the crowd. It was well known that his one abiding wish was to be relieved of this tiring command and to once again enter Rome's campaign to acquire, by force, land far north of Rome, in the cold mountains, so that he could once again claim the prestige of seemingly being in charge of something, something of value. Not this.

Pilate continued addressing the guards immediately around him in a tone of self-pity and growing frustration. "This heat—it makes me crazy. Something odious is in the air." He then turned abruptly to the crowd and entreated rather than ordered them, "Take him yourselves and try him by your own law." Jesus now seemed to be in more trouble than even he could have imagined.

But the people shouted back that Rome had taken the law from them and from the Sanhedrin. The power to crucify, or otherwise punish, any prisoners was no longer theirs. Stoning was still a sanctioned form of execution, but not crucifixion. Rome had decided to reserve this excruciating death for themselves alone, especially for doing away with mere slaves. Now Pilate acknowledged to himself, perhaps, by the confused look on his face, what a mistake that was. He had been put in the unfortunate position of having to abide by Rome's own decree.

Stalling, he continued his interrogation: "Why do you work on the Sabbath? Did you raise a man from the dead? Did you drive money changers out of the temple? Who are you to forgive people? What are you doing with the poor? Why are you with prostitutes? Where are all your disciples? Do you have an army?" A strange urgency now packed his questions. It was as if he followed some agreed-upon protocol to end the pain of what felt like a public humiliation. He no longer paused even long enough for the tortured face before him to respond in his exhausted whispers.

Clearly impatient and self-conscious in front of all the people, who were straining to hear his words even while shouting their own desires at him, Pilate rubbed his hands together in a vague gesture, as if ridding them of dirt or some abhorrent matter. Pilate then asked the Nazarene if he had any response to the number of charges leveled against him. I knew that Jesus's silence was what drove Pilate and the crowd into a raging madness. Never had I heard silence used so powerfully as a response. All the charges hurled at him—though vague and unsupported—were effectively deflected with silence. His silence actually rose up above the sounds of the crowd and the mock interrogation to cover the entire Praetorium. Frustrated, the crowd grew quiet in order to hear Jesus's answers. It was clear that his silence was driving the crowd, as well as Pilate, mad. I could see it on their faces. He had checked their bogus form of justice with a weapon stronger than their own: silence itself, which indicted all those on the stage who were ready to condemn the beaten man. This did not go unnoticed by Pilate and his guards, and they began to murmur nervously among themselves.

A man next to me, wearing an old and tattered robe, cried out to Jesus, "Why don't you answer? What do you have to lose?"

Jesus's head turned slightly, as if he were mildly interested in the question, but he remained silent. It seemed as though Jesus saw into the faces of the people in the crowd as well. Why else did he look so patiently upon their rage and fear? It was not that their shouts for his death didn't affect him. At times, I saw him visibly cringe when a loud member of the crowd demanded that Pilate condemn him to death. And it was obvious that the Roman leader was pleased he had manipulated the support of the crowd toward his decision. Pilate would further consolidate his power over any possible insurrection under his rule.

I turned my attention to the accuser. I refused to be caught up in the crowd's purposeless ways. Some unknown Nazarene could not swerve me away from my intentions. He was helpless. I wasn't. I had my life to give. It would be for the death of those who had killed Pricilla and taken my son from me. I grasped the handle of my knife once again. All this talk about Jesus would need to be ignored. I had to attend to what mattered. I needed to get myself in a position to carry out what every step of the way to Jerusalem had told me—and my grief and anger had filled me with the power to do. My knife would settle matters once and for all. I just needed the chance.

IX

I now intended, at whatever cost to myself, to give the Romans back a small taste of the bitterness they had required me to swallow. Pilate would not suspect me. Albus might even come into the crowd as one of his guards. If so, I'd go for him first. The Romans, by way of Pilate, would pay for their lustful violence that had killed Pricilla. Better yet that it was Albus!

Soon Pilate would move close enough for me to reach him in a few steps. I'd deliver my knife to his heart and that of every Roman responsible for the death of my wife. A sense of calm came over me. My thoughts sharpened like the edge of the blade hidden in my robe.

I kept my focus on Pilate. I watched his every move. Annoyingly, Jesus, who now stood before him, kept distracting me. I resented the attention Jesus took, and I kept trying to block him out of my mind, focusing exactly on where I would stab Pilate.

Pilate was still questioning Jesus. Now, however, he asked a question of Jesus and then turned to the crowd. The crowd began to chant back answers for Jesus. Pilate asked, "Do you think you're a king?" There was no response from Jesus.

The crowd, however, chanted back, "He does. He does." They followed their chanting with laughter and loud shouts, while the people in the crowd sometimes swayed in one accord in their judgment of Jesus.

Unfortunately, Jesus's silence distracted me even more than if he had been angry as well. Why didn't he defend himself? Pilate was now more interested in the crowd than in Jesus or the prisoner I heard someone call Barabbas. They were incidental to Pilate's desire to appease the restlessness of Jerusalem through giving the crowd what it wanted.

Meanwhile, Jesus refused to speak, so Pilate turned abruptly and addressed the crowd. Sarcastically, he asked them, "And what would you have me do with him?"

"Crucify! Crucify him!" they shouted back.

I could not fathom their brutal response. That the authorities were willing to follow this mindless crowd only illustrated the powerlessness of Rome. This man in front of them, stripped and bleeding, wearing a mock kingly crown painfully penetrating his skull with thorns, who would soon die on this very day, showed in his silence a strength of will and character that the Sanhedrin, the legions of soldiers, Caiaphas, and Pilate himself could surely not even imagine. And neither could I. I did not understand this power.

Yet in spite of their cruelty, Jesus seemed to absorb their vehemence as though enfolded in some mystery beyond their comprehension. This seemed to annoy the crowd further. The mysterious elements of this brutalized man were hidden from the blind passion of the crowd, as though buried in the furrows of his wounds.

A wave of confusion suddenly passed through me. Who was this man? I needed clarity at the moment, not confusion. Yet looking at Jesus, I saw that he exuded a unique power, and it unsettled me. I could feel its affect on the crowd as well. Maybe it was fear I felt. Did I doubt that I could do what I had intended since leaving Cyrene?

My heart began to race. A cold sweat broke out on my forehead. My knife in place? Yes. I touched it once again. The time had come. Clearly about to release one of the two prisoners, either Jesus or the man called Barabbas, Pilate called them both forward and ordered them to stand facing the crowd. Barabbas stood with a defiant look, while Jesus kept his head down and reluctantly moved forward ... toward the masses before him.

To my right, and still in front of Pilate's judgment seat, a commotion suddenly erupted. A dozen soldiers had quickly stepped in front of the crowd. They had surrounded the same young woman I'd seen before, the one with the long black hair, standing near her parents. Immediately, I knew. She was meant for the prisoner's pleasures. I had to get close to her. I quickly moved to my right and slipped forward through the crowd, not far from her.

The young girl's mother was weeping. Her father stood with arms crossed and an angry scowl on his face. I could only imagine their thoughts at surrendering their daughter to a prisoner. Yet by morning, she would be free, free of the prisoner, free of Pilate. But first she would yield to some unknown brutal prisoner who was to be released by Pilate. And I was sure that Barabbas would likely be the one released, not Jesus. Although she would soon be free from the dirty fingers of Pilate, the young girl was visibly shaking. Strangely, she appeared focused mostly on Jesus.

The soldiers were near her but trying not to draw much attention. As if those in the crowd knew what was happening, they formed a small circle around the young girl and her parents. No one was inclined to interfere.

I quickly moved even closer to the girl, until only her parents were between her and me. Without drawing attention to myself, I slipped my right hand under my cloak and firmly grasped the handle of my knife. I waited now only for the moment when Pilate would come down from the platform and personally release the prisoner, no doubt the one called Barabbas, to the young girl.

Pilate called a few guards forward and ordered them to secure the prisoners, Jesus and Barabbas, although it was unlikely that either one had any chance of escape. As part of Pilate's show for the crowd, the guards marched forward in formation and positioned themselves around the two prisoners.

I watched Pilate. He gathered his robe about himself, and with a sweep of his left arm over the crowd, he began to descend the stairs from the elevated platform. Soon I would drive my knife as deeply as I could into the heart of this tyrant.

And then it happened. The unexpected suddenly happened. Pilate's wife appeared near the platform. She handed a note to a guard, who moved quickly to Pilate and gave it to him.

Pilate stopped talking. He stopped halfway down the staircase and reached out for a nearby railing. Whatever the note said, it had a profound effect on him. Immediately silent, he glanced toward his wife. Some dark emotion—what I thought was fear—crossed his face.

He continued his descent, then hesitated and returned to the platform. He stood in front of Jesus and Barabbas, while loudly dismissing the guards who reluctantly retreated from the scene.

My heart sank like a huge stone dropped into the bottom of our well in Cyrene. I realized that Pilate was not coming toward me, not coming into the crowd. Somehow, his wife had interfered with her husband's yearly ritual. I didn't know why. Something in the note ... whatever it was.

I watched in disbelief as the young woman and her parents fled into the crowd. Pilate recalled the guards standing near them. No attempt followed to pursue them. I released my hold on my knife. I glanced around to see if anyone, especially any of the soldiers, had seen me. I didn't see anyone looking at me. I felt numb as I stared once again at Pilate while catching a glimpse of his wife slipping away into the palace. She had ruined my moment with a mysterious note to her husband.

I could do nothing. I stood staring in disbelief, and something folded within me like the sudden collapse of a tent. I had to watch the scene unfold, although I hardly took in what I saw. Everything appeared to slow before me. I simply gave in to the pushing and shoving crowd. I had no power to resist while I watched what continued to happen.

Barabbas still stood on one side of Pilate, Jesus on the other. What a contrast! Barabbas, a condemned, defiant criminal. The other, Jesus of Nazareth, already wounded, head slightly bowed, standing in the silence of his own making.

"And who shall I release?" Pilate now shouted to the crowd.

"Barabbas ... Barabbas!" they shouted without hesitation.

"Then you shall have Barabbas," Pilate replied, raising his eyebrows, a slight smile crossing his face. Released, Barabbas raised his fist in triumph and rushed into the cheering crowd.

Shaking, I reached for my knife again. I began to scan the faces of the soldiers. Surely Abenadar or Albus must be here somewhere. They must be members of this palace guard. But where were they?

Grasping my knife, I remembered Justin, how playfully he'd asked to see my knife. Another toy. I almost pulled it out of my cloak as though to hand it to him. My mind seemed to be running away from me and into the crowd. I couldn't believe I was so close to striking Pilate in the heart, and now I was so far away. Hardly able to control my shaking, I wondered if it was visible to those around me. For a moment, as though suddenly thrown into a dream, I imagined I had killed Pilate. No, not far from me, he stood alongside Jesus.

Now what would I do? I didn't know.

Pilate turned to the crowd. "And now what would you have me do with this man, this Jesus of Nazareth?"

Without hesitation, the crowd shouted, "Crucify! Crucify him!"

Pilate took a few steps backward. His face betrayed surprise and confusion. He seemed not to be expecting such persistence out of this mob below him, speaking now in one voice. Fearful of not really appeasing the bloodlust of the crowd, but knowing in his heart—I can only guess—that executing the man in front of him did not fit the crime, Pilate exonerated himself and pleased the fickle rabble all in one gesture.

He said to the crowd in a mocking tone, "Here is your king. Take him away!"

The crowd shouted again, even louder, "Crucify him!"

Pilate's carefully planned drama had begun to spin away from him. So had mine. His wife had taken the knife out of my hand and out of the heart of her husband. By her unexpected appearance, she had simply thwarted my plan for revenge. Pilate's wife had interrupted his amusement at releasing one of his playthings to the released prisoner. In a subtle way, by delivering some message to him, she had, intentionally or otherwise, unraveled a thread in Pilate's ongoing tapestry of infidelity to her. One of his amusements had been exposed, and Pilate had been exposed as well.

Now Pilate turned his anger toward the crowd and began to play Jesus against them. He played with the crowd. "Do you want me to crucify your king?" he asked in a scornful tone, drawing out the word "king."

With that, the chief priests got into the act as well. A few of them shouted, "We have no king except Caesar."

Pilate had one of his servants bring him a bowl of water. With an exaggerated gesture that everyone could see, he dipped his hands into the water and proclaimed to the crowd, "I am innocent of this man's blood. It is your doing."

To which the crowd responded, "Let his blood be on us and on our children."

The trial was over. Pilate handed Jesus over to a special contingent of soldiers. I scanned the guards for Abenadar or Albus once again, but it was in vain, for the soldiers seemed to blur together before me. Jesus was silent. The crowd had grown quiet as well.

I was still transfixed by what had happened within the last few moments. Pilate stood before me alive and well. I was still alive. I would see Justin again. I'd soon figure out something else. For now, I just had to get out of the ugly crowd and away from this strange man from the town of Nazareth. I also had to get away from Pilate. I'd had enough of his unpredictable and interfering wife, who had, in a few simple moments, robbed me of my revenge.

I'd lost my chance for revenge, or so I thought.

X

Like a sudden ebbing of the sea, I felt exhausted. The unexpected turn of events resulting in my failure to revenge the death of Pricilla and my imprisoned son had left me empty. I just wanted to get away, out of the crowd, out of a feeling of failure. I didn't know what to do next.

Much to my surprise, when I looked at Jesus again, I was reminded of Pricilla. Their agonizing images blurred before my eyes. For a moment, I couldn't separate them. I couldn't sort out their suffering. Both were the subjects of cruel and uncalled-for violence. It felt so senseless, and I watched Jesus being flogged by a tall, muscular soldier without his helmet, who continued to lash Jesus and then look to the crowd for approval.

Seeing Jesus, I sighed deeply. When I looked at the sight of this poor man, so intent and so alert to all that was happening, and yet being publicly scourged, I had to turn away. The noise of the crowd brought me back to what was happening.

It was as though the crowd's very security was threatened by the fate of this Nazarene. If he didn't die, Rome's power would be weakened, and Pilate would lose face with the people once again. The crowd's fear that no one was ultimately in charge would create even more chaos. Rome would be shown to be weak at its core. On the other hand, there was no obvious power in this strange man called Jesus. Maybe that was what was so infuriating—the fact that there was a power present that neither the crowd, by what I could surmise, nor myself could grasp. How could we trust the power of someone seemingly absorbing hatred with unswerving compassion for those around him?

Instead, the crowd's hatred had become a source of security, and I felt drawn into everyone's anger, though it seemed strange to me as well. They had unified their wills. They seemed to feel their collective power to exert some influence. It was life to them, and they were visibly intoxicated with this new power. They were waiting for Pilate to echo back their hatred. I could only conjecture, but the crowd appeared desperate to hear Pilate order the soldiers to take Jesus away and crucify him, as though those orders would give them some relief.

For an instant, I had a strange thought: of myself being condemned to crucifixion. Along with the thought came a wonderful feeling of relief—an ending to it all, to the grief and emptiness, to the daily routine. I wished in my heart to change lives with Jesus, to carry my own cross to my own hill and experience a painful yet merciful death.

Yet how could I think this?

Maybe I was entangled in the emotions of the crowd. Perhaps that's what the crowd was trying to do. Maybe it was trying to kill something in itself through killing this Nazarene. If he could only die, maybe they could get rid of their haunting fears of their own deaths. Replace him for us. Kill something through him. Kill this helplessness before Rome. Kill our own powerlessness before death. These thoughts terrified me while simultaneously attracting me to some wonderful oblivion. Perhaps all this pain inside of me would finally die.

Yet something in me knew I could not simply imitate him. I was not on trial. Jesus was not Pricilla. How had they mingled together in my mind? Why was all this blurring before me? Somehow, it seemed designed to drive me to some other unfamiliar place in my life. Grasping for some reasonableness, I told myself I would have to live my own life. I'd have to go through my own death, not in his way, but in my way. I could not escape the sense that this man Jesus of Nazareth was showing me a way, some path that I had never seen before, and that his own violent death had crossed my own in a most unexpected way.

Another guard now began to flog Jesus. The crowd watched intently. A few began to imitate some soldiers who occasionally called out a mocking chant, "Hail, king of the Jews! Hail, king of the Jews!"

One guard looked into Christ's face and spat a wad of green spit into it. The others sneered at such a vile act, but no one repeated it, for it seemed to shock even some of them. Even the guard drew back from his own act, clearly bewildered by what he had done, looking around for some sign of approval from others. Receiving none, he looked even more puzzled at his sudden act of spitefulness.

While it was apparent that they thought it clever and humorous for Christ to wear the scarlet robe of Rome, they were certainly not going to let him wear it in public, lest they themselves be shamed by it. So the soldiers stripped him of it and put his filthy robes back on him, preparing to lead him out for crucifixion.

"Best to be done with him … as soon as we can," stated the leader of a new group of soldiers gathered around Jesus. He was a small, heavy man who seemed lost in his armor. He spoke with authority, plainly knowing Pilate was closely watching him, for he often looked at him. Assigned to carry out the execution, they all would be lashed as well if they failed to get the prisoner alive to Golgotha for the crucifixion that Pilate now had a special interest in seeing carried out swiftly. Clearly, the fickle crowd's wishes had disturbed him.

Pilate merely nodded to the leader he addressed as Gustus. The cross lying at the base of the platform was picked up by two guards and placed roughly on the back of Jesus, which immediately bowed him down under its weight. The procession began to move forward. Jesus took a few hesitant steps and stumbled, but he was able to catch himself before he fell and before the heavy wooden cross crushed him.

"Kill the bastard," a man growled at Jesus as he was led away. I hardly heard his words because Jesus passed so close to me that his soiled and bloodstained robe seemed almost within reach. Yet why would I reach for him?

As Jesus passed me and others standing close to him, a hush suddenly fell over us. His face was so swollen that it was hard to distinguish its features. Several of us could only shake our heads. Jesus stumbled again. Two soldiers prodded him with spears. Three others soldiers on horses pushed the crowd back with short charges into the crowed while leading the small procession away from the Praetorioum toward the hill called Golgotha—meaning "the place of a skull."

The hush of the crowd as Jesus passed us left behind a strange silence. It was a silence I had been fleeing since Pricilla's death—escaping until this moment. When I'd awakened in the arms of Rufus and realized Pricilla had died, a terrible stillness had suddenly entered my life. I hated the silence that had pulled her away from me. And here it was again. A silence enveloped this Nazarene and now me. I didn't know what to make of it. I was hardly a criminal, not yet at least, nor was I being led away, condemned to die. What did this Jesus have to do with me?

A busy scene was now unfolding before me. There were the harsh commands of the few Roman soldiers pushing the staggering prisoner forward, only to see him stumble, be taunted, and prodded to go forward. The prisoner kept struggling to stay on his feet.

I began to follow not far behind Jesus. In addition to many in the original crowd at his trial, a few others began to gather along the road. A few of the younger ones ran toward the city gate to be ready when the prisoner reached them. I heard some wagering that he would not make it that far.

In fact, the execution, so vehemently and savagely called for by the crowd and agreed to by Pilate, was now in danger of a dull ending. The prisoner might die before being crucified. What would they say of Pilate's handling of this case back in Caesarea? Those nearest to Jesus were shouting at him to keep going.

Even the guards saw what was happening. I heard one shout to his companion, "He's bleeding too much! We really worked him over. He'll never make it."

"It'll be our heads," his companion replied.

Another soldier spoke up. "Not with the cross. He can't make it with the cross. It's too much. Too heavy."

Jesus now stumbled and fell. The crossbeam hitting the cobbled street sent a loud crack echoing off the surrounding walls.

I could take no more. I turned to make my way back through the crowd. I had begun to walk against the crowd and could see their faces transfixed by the procession continuing down the narrow walled street. I wanted to get home as soon as possible and forget the day, so I quickened my pace.

Suddenly, a thick hand grabbed me by the shoulder and spun me around. I turned to face the fat, round face of Gustus spitting out orders at me: "Not so fast there! Where do you think you're going? I command you to carry his cross!"

XI

❁

I was shocked by Gustus's order. I impulsively slipped my hand through the pocket of my robe to feel for my knife. The commander didn't notice, for the people in the crowd that had quickly gathered around us appeared to be a distraction. He was no Abenadar, no Albus, though the sight of his armor reminded me once again of the four Roman soldiers riding up to our home. If I couldn't have them, perhaps I could kill Gustus and then escape in the crowd. There was no escaping his command, though. I knew what it meant. A Roman soldier could compel any of us to do his bidding. Resisting such a command was sure punishment—if not sudden death.

I would not let myself be killed. The only reason I would die was to avenge the death of my wife and the abduction of my oldest son. Albus was the one who had killed her. I took my hand away from my knife in the hopes it would not be taken from me.

A few more soldiers joined Gustus, dispersing the crowd around me and pushing me toward where Jesus lay on the ground, not far from a bloodied cross.

One young soldier, with a barrel-like chest and broad shoulders, pushed me forward. He bent down under the crux of the cross, quickly lifted it up, and dropped it across my back. My knees gave in under its weight, and I let out a groan as I felt its impact.

"There you go," said Gustus. "A little something for you to carry." Then he laughed, walked around in front of me, and asked, "Where are you from?"

I said, "Cyrene."

"And your name?"

"Simon."

"Okay," he said. "Simon of Cyrene, follow the prisoner." And then Gustus turned, waddled away, and I saw him being helped onto his horse.

Out of the corner of my eye, I glimpsed Jesus. He had turned his swollen face slightly toward me to see what had happened, and for a moment, our eyes met.

I turned away. Why had I been chosen to do this? I resented Jesus's look. I did not understand it. It wasn't despair. He wasn't giving up. He was painfully suffering. For what? I wasn't there to figure it out. I had another task to accomplish. I had to find Abenadar and Albus. I had no time for the man called Jesus, or for carrying a cross for Rome. Yet I saw no escape. Not from him. Not from the cross. Not yet.

The smell of fresh blood from Jesus penetrated my nostrils. I shifted my head from the smell of the cross. Old blood mingled with the blood of Jesus. This wasn't the first time this cross had been used to cruelly execute a criminal. Perhaps as many as a dozen men had been crucified on it in the recent past.

"King of the Jews, get up now. Your helper is here. All you have to do is walk. A king should be able to do that," a soldier called out to Jesus, laughing to himself.

Jesus struggled to his feet and began to walk not far in front of me. I refused to look at all of him. I saw only the heels of his bloody feet shuffling along on the stone street. I had my own task: getting used to the weight of the cross.

Disinterested in their day's assignment, the soldiers next to me were clearly more at ease after having escaped the eyes of Pilate. Jesus, to these men, was one more bloody body to be affixed to the wood and left to die, another incidental human being to be put into a pauper's grave or claimed by those who knew him.

The Passover festival would be kept quiet. The release of Barabbas had served its purpose. Perhaps, as Rufus said, other prisoners would be selectively released around Jerusalem once Pilate saw that the Passover festival would present no rebellions. I knew from my many conversations with Rufus and Alexander that this was how Rome intimidated us Jews. It systematically kept its oppressive hold on the people in a growing atmosphere of resentment and rebellion, checked only by the fear of torture. Pilate had his informers, and he especially watched the synagogues, in particular the one built for the Cyreneans, who so often traveled to Jerusalem, and who traded with Cyrene by land and sea. They were often the most restless, the most radical. An uprising might well start there, and Alexander had been known to be a leader among the Cyrenean synagogue.

A chilling thought shuddered through my body. Could Pilate have ordered Abenadar to follow my sons to our home, kill their mother, and make my sons watch? I dismissed the thought. Surely it was the random hatred and lust of a few renegade soldiers that had killed her. Killing Pricilla hadn't been planned. But had the capture of Alexander been part of the systematic plan to ensure a peaceful Passover?

My sons saw their own mother suffer and die, while I could do nothing. How would they ever forget? Rufus refused to talk more about what he had seen. I could only imagine the horror that lay embedded in his life. Alexander would suffer as well if he was still alive. It all seemed so senseless. What made sense was getting back at Rome—at least at the soldiers who had killed my wife, especially Abenadar or Albus. Those I would recognize in a moment, the scarred-faced one and the one with the mangled tongue.

As I began walking along behind Jesus, the haunting feeling that nothing mattered anymore mingled with the smell of blood warmed by the late morning sun. My wife had died. Now another death of a seemingly innocent man was about to occur. Who cared? I was walking without purpose. I had to get over the feeling. I was more than my feelings. I had to get back to my task. Somewhere in Jerusalem, I would soon find Abenadar and Albus.

Nonetheless, though worse for wear, the cross I carried was still fully usable. Multiple spike holes filled the beam of the cross. At times, I found myself counting them. A line of criminals had died on this cross. It was a line that I easily could have joined only a little while ago, had I been able to get to Pilate. How thin was the line between the bitterness in my heart and the actions of those who ended up crucified on this cross? Yet what had this man done? Why him? And why, of all the people in that crowd, had they chosen me for this miserable task?

Haunted by the question, I couldn't walk away from it. I carried it on my back.

The pavement was wet from the light rain that had fallen the night before. The smell of blood on the moistened wood continued to fill my nostrils and mingle with the sweat and blood of the Nazarene, penetrating the cross he could no longer manage to carry for himself. I fought back the nausea and weakness that overcame me. I knew that now my own life was unsafe. If I could, I had to find a way out of this.

My ruminating kept being interrupted by the weight of the cross pressing into my shoulder. My sandals slipped on the wet stones. I almost fell. The shoulder I had injured as a boy began to ache. I had fallen from an olive tree and hurt it, and it had never completely healed. It gave me pain every time I lifted my arm directly over my head, or when I had to carry something on my shoulder. Now I felt the pain again. What a difference between those peaceful old olive groves and this bloody poplar that I was being asked to carry for the one condemned, the one they called Jesus. How did I get from there to here? It made no sense.

Why couldn't I just ask Gustus to get someone else? I'd do this for some time and then put in my request. Didn't I have enough to deal with? Didn't anyone know that I had just buried my wife? Let someone else help. I needed help. I could slip back into the crowd's anonymous security and be done with this task. The thought of being relieved of this burden—his cross, not mine—before reaching Golgotha strengthened me. At least I could carry it part of the way.

The right side of my head rested up against the wet poplar, and I could feel my right shoulder fit into the crux of the cross. I snuggled my shoulder farther into the space where the crossbeam met the vertical beam in order to gain a better hold on it.

Nausea, some strange sickness, began to settle in me. A few people from the crowd seemed to want to walk fairly near me. There were several women, a beggar, a man apparently tormented by demons ...

He suddenly shouted out, "Heal me, Jesus. Please heal me."

Jesus stopped, searching for the voice in the crowd lining the street. Immediately, Gustus rode up, put his horse between Jesus and the crowd, and shouted, "None of that! You've done enough of that. Keep moving!" The people in the crowd mostly kept their distance, and yet they seemed to want to follow the procession. I would have thought I'd feel more conspicuous than I did. The pain in my shoulder kept me from feeling the eyes of the crowd, which seemed outright hostile. Was I depriving them of seeing Jesus suffer even more?

"He's a friend of the Nazarene; crucify him as well!" shouted one man with a deep scar on the right side of his face. A soldier quickly rode his horse toward the man and drove him back into the crowd.

I said nothing. I didn't want attention, yet another man close by began to point at me. "He's a follower. Let's find his followers."

"Crucify them … get rid of them all," echoed his partner. It was obvious that both had been drinking heavily, and they were laughing heartily at their bravado.

Murmurs of growing support for their suggestion reached my ears, and surely Jesus's, at the same time. Fear crept into my feet, up my body and across to my right shoulder, and down into my heart. Perhaps I was in more danger than I'd thought. I could simply drop the cross and run. I could take my chances with the Romans and their whips. Perhaps I too was walking toward my inevitable end. Having my own wife die with such cruelty pushed me into what I did know but wanted to deny. My own end was not a matter of whether, but of when. Yet this was Jesus's death. Not mine.

Suddenly Jesus seemed to slow on purpose. With a few steps, I was alongside him. He reached out for me and pressed his hand onto my left shoulder. I could only turn my head a little way to the left because the crossbeam held me straight. Unexpectedly, for a moment I felt the weight of the cross lift. Even my nausea passed.

A soldier quickly rode up and pushed Jesus forward, in front of me once again. Close to him for a moment, I had seen how deeply he was suffering the pain of his death march. I had joined his walk to Golgotha. Jesus had entirely surrendered to what was happening. Most people looked away from him when they got close. It was as though they thought they were immune from the consequences of his journey if only they stayed to the side of the street and remained unmoved by his passing. How foolish. Did the people in the crowd really think they were not part of this march as well?

I began to look more closely at the crowd lining the narrow streets.

Most of the more vehement and hostile men and women had lagged behind, as if finding their previous source of amusement no longer interesting. I saw new faces. I saw for the first time the looks of painful recognition that some tragedy was unfolding before them. Some seemed shaken and visibly covered their faces as he passed. I even saw a few women with tears in their eyes, shaking their heads in disbelief. I didn't know what to make of this. I hadn't sensed that he had much of a following at all, yet suddenly he had many there to help him on his way, help him by just being there on his lonely path ahead.

From a hunkered stance beneath the cross, I looked out at the crowd of women, children, men dressed well and others in rags, and still others who were invalids—blind, crippled, poor, and those missing limbs, those who crawled because their legs would not support them. Some scorned Jesus. Others reached out to touch his bloody, torn garment. What became clear to me instantly was that the surrender of Jesus had somehow pulled so many of us into his march toward Golgotha. None of us were really bystanders, as I had considered myself. Even the people who lined the streets to watch us pass seemed compelled to join the procession.

Had these people gone mad? They seemed to be swept into the march itself, as though whatever their condition, the presence of Jesus was so large that it included more and more of those lining the streets. A strange sense of unreality, or of some other reality, noticeably began to engulf the entire procession. What was happening? I even found myself distracted from my obsession with my own intentions, and I fought back the feeling that what I was doing had more importance than one more common execution.

Yet Jesus, with no visible effort, seemed to be drawing us into another realm, though there was no effort for it to happen. As I looked at him, the numerous parables I'd heard of him telling flashed through my mind. This other realm he talked about in parables about grains of wheat, children, pearls lost, tiny mustard seeds ... He seemed to have become before us a living parable himself of this other world, this other way of living through his horrible suffering. It was as though this innocent man was stirring in us a world that even now we entered as we walked with him toward his death. For some, his presence was more than they could stand. They fought against him, renouncing him bitterly. I too felt the resentment at being required in the midst of my own suffering to serve some stranger who spoke of a world other than this one. Yet I could not escape the feeling that this cross was already bearing a mystery that I did not understand.

I told myself to just keep putting one foot in front of the other. Soon it would be over. I'd be out of whatever was happening. My mind would regain its clarity. Jesus would be gone. Out of my life. He'd be gone for good.

Once again, I began to feel rage at what was unfolding before my eyes. I wanted to hurt someone. I wished for the strength to hurl this cross into the crowd, to nail every last one of the people to it—two, no, three deep, with long spikes—and then hoist them up to hang and die. I'd tear them down in death and keep crucifying others, one after another. I wanted to do to them what some blind force had done to me in suddenly taking Pricilla from my life, and from my two sons.

I wanted out, out of the procession, away from the helpless, staggering, strange man with a clear gaze that cut so deeply into us. Where were we going, anyway? Some meaningless place of death? What was this all leading to? Could we laugh, love, and throw our lives so deeply into each other, only to have it all end on this tortured path to Golgotha?

For a time as we walked along, I tried to shut myself off from the noise of the crowd lining the stress; some people simply pressed against the walls that seemed almost leaning in upon us. I wanted to stop the procession altogether. I wanted Pricilla to please, please come to me again. I began to hate the weight placed upon me. I began to loathe Jesus's weakness. "I would crucify him myself, right now," I groaned to the street.

I looked up and saw a tall building not far ahead. I imagined that I'd lean Jesus up against the building and head out of this city. I'd never return. The dead be damned! I wanted back into the world of the living! Yet how could I come back without Pricilla? I was not ready to live while she had died. I had to find someone to blame, not for every little thing, but for the whole mess. If I killed her attackers, perhaps I would die as well—then it would all be over.

I looked ahead at Jesus, who continued to stagger along ahead of me. He seemed so useless. He was another Jew. And we Jews were powerless. Rome's kingdom ruled in a cruel and arbitrary way. Rome mocked our beliefs and rubbed our beards in Caesar's wishes. It had the power, and this Nazarene was one more weak prophet who couldn't help us any more than I could help Pricilla when the Roman soldiers threw themselves on her and tried to open her up with their violent desire.

If Jesus could see so well into our world, what was he thinking? What was he doing coming up to Jerusalem when he knew the authorities and religious leaders had been lying in wait for him? How smart was that? If he had a cause, how smart was it to end up dying without fulfilling it? How naive could he be?

As I began to tire even more, I felt an utter disdain for Jesus getting himself into this deadly situation. Because of his foolishness, I was carrying the cross of his own stupid choices. I hated his weakness.

The march took on a life of its own, and it seemed we were all numbed to our tasks as we moved along. I heard the grating of the wood where the vertical beam continually scraped the stones of the street. I felt its rough and persistent weight biting into my shoulder. Again, I smelled the rain, the wood, and the blood from other men long since crucified, dead, and buried.

For a moment, the procession stopped. Two soldiers chased an unruly member of the crowd into a nearby building and returned with him. In that moment, Jesus turned and gazed at me. He must have heard me called Simon because he suddenly spoke to me. "Simon of Cyrene, I need your help to fulfill my purpose."

I nodded my head, finding it hard to look away from this suffering person. I suddenly knew that he saw my fear. I had the strange sensation that he was looking at me from another world, near and yet far away.

For a moment, it seemed that both Jesus and I had crossed over into that realm, while not denying the tragedy of where we were, and that doing so made something else possible. I was not sure about that world. It was a realm of small account, made up of tiny seeds and lost sheep and coins and loaves and fishes. The cross I was carrying also belonged to this other realm. It was a place where peace was stronger than violence, where silence lived deeper than words, and where acceptance was mightier than rejection. His stories, from what I gathered, were about a deeper abundance than what we had or didn't have, especially for the poor and those cast aside, into the shadows of our world.

When he looked at me from that place, I thought for a moment that I could see this hidden kingdom, hidden from the brutality of Pilate, the crowd, Roman law and the soldiers, and even my own rage that had so abruptly seized me. I also had the thought that my dear wife must also be included in the place where he was now seeing my struggle with grief and fear and uncontrolled anger.

Strangely, in his looking at me, I saw that Pricilla was fine, even in death. In the moment following, when Jesus saw me struggle for his sake, I tightened my grip on the crossbeam. I placed one hand over the other, and with more certainty, I committed myself to going on. Meanwhile, the fleeting thought that I might relieve some of Jesus's struggle helped support the heavy beams on my shoulder. The cross was infused with life, as though its weight varied. It had begun to interfere with my clear, logical plans. I could not let that continue to happen. My own purposeful revenge could not be muddled by thoughts about this Nazarene, whatever Jesus meant by fulfilling his own purpose.

XII

It was midmorning, and the hot sun caused most people to seek shade. Animals crowded the narrow passages as we made our way through the streets. Merchants hawked their wares. Women drove their best bargains but paused briefly as we passed close to them.

"He casts out demons!" I heard a woman shriek, while those around her turned to look at Jesus staggering by them. They quickly returned to their shopping. For some, not much was happening. A man being crucified. Buy some figs.

Others seemed curious as we passed them by. "Who is he?" they asked.

"I don't know," came the reply. "Another criminal. He'll get his due."

Narrow streets made it easy to hear the throngs along our path. At times, I could just about hear people whisper as I passed them by.

Some were curious about me. I heard a young girl ask her mother, "Is he going to die too?"

"I don't know," she said. "Perhaps. He looks like a criminal. Get back against the wall," she ordered her daughter, and in moments we had left them behind. I began to wonder if I was not condemned as well in some strange twist of fate. How had I entered this parade of death? I guess when I was born. Sooner or later, I'd reach my end as well.

How dramatically things had changed within a few short hours. I had come for revenge, yet I was pressed into service, service to Rome, service to a stranger, Jesus, who was having a strange effect on me. Thoughts and vivid scenes about life had me more than I had them, and they were falling outside the boundaries of my usual reasonable approach to solving difficulties.

Perhaps it was the sun now beating incessantly down on me. I'm not sure. I couldn't think straight, as if a dream had enveloped me. I couldn't escape. I wasn't my dream. It was not a dream I had. The dream had me. Now it was being extended into this strange daylight march, and the clear, bright, rational sun could not chase it away. The Nazarene had enveloped me in a dream that was foreign to the world I knew.

The bloody cross pressed harder against my shoulder. So much for being ritually pure for the Passover festival. No chance of that. And what was pure about this death march? I began to feel the cross's terrible weight again. If I strained to lift my head, I could see Jesus. Sometimes he moved forward in a straight line. Then, moments later, he would veer from one side to another as though drunk on new wine. Someone even shouted out, "He's a friend of drunkards!"

"No," said another. "He likes prostitutes better. He thinks nothing of forgiving them. Corrupts us all."

From the other side of the street I heard an old man simply say, "I know he loves the poor. There're so many of us."

The weight of the cross now weakened me. My shoulders stooped and my gait slowed. Perhaps I seemed guilty myself. A few people began to mock me as well. Sweat poured off my forehead and fell before me. Dung covered my sandals. Surrounded by angry men, and some women, from all over the region, and soldiers who would as soon beat me to death as look at me, I began to fear I couldn't continue. What would Rufus, Yiska, and Nava think if they came upon me now? If only Alexander were free, he'd find a way to get me out of this mess.

Jesus shuffled his bare feet along the street, only a short distance ahead. My head down, I could follow his trail of blood drops. I tried to avoid stepping on his blood smeared here and there on the cobbled street. When the wind shifted, I could smell his unwashed and sweaty body, a pungent, slightly fetid, and sweet odor. Sweat, mixed with blood from the sharp thorns encircling his head, dripped down the back of his neck. I did not understand how he kept staggering forward. People jeered at his appearance, and from time to time picked up the chant, "Hail, king of the Jews!"

Jesus had to be at the edge of what his body could endure. I saw no unusual physical strength in him. I occasionally caught a glimpse of his bruised face when he turned a bit to look at the crowds lining the street. Once I saw him look directly into the eyes of a young boy, perhaps thirteen or fourteen years old. The boy returned his gaze. I could see Jesus's face suddenly soften before he turned and looked ahead once more.

Perhaps no one else noticed this simple exchange. There was nothing impressive about him now. His wounded body had driven his spirit inward. Apparently absorbing the necessity of his death as we moved along, he appeared to look in vain for a little comfort from someone in the crowds of people. Mostly people mocked him, although on occasion I saw men and women stunned into silence. Jesus showed no outward sign of resistance to the inevitable journey toward Golgotha. He did not resist in any show of defiance or particular heroism. Nor did he simply collapse out of terror and give in as I had once heard a young man had done. The young man had to be bound, knocked out, and carried to his execution.

Who could blame Jesus if he did the same? No, Jesus did not seem to anticipate so much what was ahead, however horrifying it seemed. He was fully absorbing what was happening to him along the way. I would never forget that. By the time I had been conscripted to carry his cross, Jesus had already borne the awful condemnation of Pilate and the crowd, and the terrible isolation and rejection by even some of his closest followers. Jesus experienced this years before. I was told that while sitting at the temple, he had experienced both loyalty and betrayal, the favor of young children, acceptance by many of the poor and rejected women who sought out his understanding of their plight. Uncertainties filled each day for him. Jesus confided once to his disciples, I was told at the temple, that even foxes had holes and birds had nests, but he had no place to rest his own head. A homeless man. While having no home, Jesus had become even more homeless when deserted by his closest followers. How was this day any different?

He also had been driven from town to town. Religious and political authorities constantly stalked him. He had been branded a troublemaker, a person disrespectful of law and order and ordinary human decency and decorum. When people feared him, they also hated him. Now those who feared him had the power to get rid of him. What no one seemed to be able to get rid of was his power to absorb their hatred and violence.

Suddenly, my thoughts were interrupted. The procession halted. A gnarled, crippled young woman was cursing Jesus. She was out of control, and a soldier pulled out his sword and took a long stride toward her just as Jesus turned to look at her. For an instant, she caught his eye and suddenly backed up, kneeling down and burying her head in her hands. She began to weep and cried out, "Jesus, Jesus of Nazareth, have mercy on me. I don't know what I'm doing. Forgive me. Please forgive me." The guard stepped between them and stood there, waiting for one of them to make a move. Neither one did. Silence surrounded the three of them, and then, strangely, she lifted her head and seemed at peace. The soldier was shocked. Quickly, in a gruff voice, he ordered the procession to move forward. I was unsure of what had happened. How had she so suddenly become so calm, even with the power of Rome standing between her and Jesus?

I began to feel dizzy and stagger from side to side. A sort of shimmering light was passing before my eyes, and I feared I'd faint. The cross felt heavier than it was moments before. I slowed my walk. I was dimly aware that Jesus had stopped, turned to a woman in the crowd, and said in a gentle yet commanding voice, "Bring Simon, the Cyrenean, some water." He nodded in my direction, and wiping the sweat out of my eyes, I could see him looking at me. He must have heard my name when I told Gustus who I was and where I lived. Yet, once again, calling me by my name startled me, as though I was hearing my name for the first time. I didn't think he knew enough to see my own plight and weakening condition.

Before the nearest guard could interfere, the woman, young and wearing fine clothing, stepped out of the crowd with a small clay pitcher of water and offered it to me. I hastily tried to drink the water while balancing the cross on my shoulder. The nearest soldier closed in on the woman, forcing her back into the crowd. She fell on the pavement, the clay pot shattering around her. The water spilled, and the guard laughed at her as she crawled on all fours into the safety of the crowd.

The water helped. I nodded toward Jesus. Still, I wondered if I could go on. Now I knew he had seen me. Called out my name. As a result, I began to see him more clearly, as though for the first time. So many stories about him, distractions for me, and yet now he was a few feet away, knowing I needed water.

What else did he know? Did he know the seething anger and grief that had broken me apart like that clay jar? Did he know that I had been thrown to the ground on all fours, just as the young woman had? I didn't know where to go. There was no safety in the crowd. Revenge had not yet purified me of my deadly purposes. I knew my revenge would cost me my own life, yet I had ceased to care. Pricilla was gone. So was Alexander. Was I trying to get rid of myself? What made me think I could kill Pilate, Abenadar, or Albus? Had I gone mad? Was I trying to kill them or kill the terrible grief I had been feeling ever since I awakened to the tragedy in our home? A deadly mistake to confuse the two!

I began to move forward once again. Water would never quench the thirst I now felt. While the path ahead blurred before me, I felt a shudder of fear when I admitted to myself that I felt lost. Carrying this cross had begun to wear me down. Somehow, this Nazarene had gotten too much in the way of what I still intended to do.

I would try to go on following this condemned man. He had called me out of an impersonal and deadly trek to Golgotha. He had called me by name, Simon of Cyrene. In doing so, he had suddenly shattered some terrible loneliness that had been thrown on my back when I had been compelled to carry his cross. I now knew I was not alone.

XIII

I now took smaller steps, trying to find a way to carry the cross more easily. The nausea was gone. I'd been forced to help this man in the last hours of his life, yet now I was willing to carry his cross for him. Unlike Gustus or the soldiers who were about to crucify him, Jesus seemed to bear no hatred toward those who had hurt him so violently. They had vented their hatred on him just as they had on Pricilla, by driving their violence into her, thinly disguised by lust.

Mysteriously, Jesus drew me along behind him, clearly distracting me from my original purpose. Maybe I needed a distraction for a while to make it to the end. He had acknowledged me by name, recognizing me as part of this journey to death. Only a short time ago, I could not imagine—with my knife in hand, ready to kill Pilate—that I would now be following this Jesus of Nazareth while my will to kill any Roman was fading. How could that be? I considered it temporary. All I had to do was to think for a moment of Albus grinding himself into my wife and then swiftly slitting her throat to Abenadar's laughter. My sons forced to watch! I would find Albus yet. Maybe not today. But soon.

Not paying attention to what was in front of me, but having fallen into a dreamy rhythm with the cross seeming to guide me through the streets toward the city gate, I almost fell across Jesus in the midst of my violent reveries. I stepped on his right foot. I realized that he had fallen on the unyielding stones patched together to lay down the semblance of a street. Jesus made no sound. There was not even a groan as his knees struck the pavement. Given the weight of the cross propelling me forward, I stopped as quickly as I could, struggling frantically to catch myself. My next impulse was to quickly put down the cross and rush to help him. The soldiers, as if anticipating my thoughts, shouted at me to stay put.

For a moment, the soldiers and the curious bystanders seemed unable to decide what to do. He hadn't tripped. He had suddenly and simply fallen heavily to the ground. Though several men had laughed, and other bystanders had let out gasps of horror, silence suddenly engulfed the moment.

Jesus's strength failed. He could not stand against all the constant forces of the earth pulling him down. As he fell, the cross suddenly felt heavier. Relieved I put it down. Only then did I begin to feel my own legs weak and trembling. So I quickly knelt on the ground, under the cross, while watching his motionless body.

A whip suddenly cracked and sliced across Jesus's back as he struggled to get up. Jesus put his palms to the stones of the street and pushed hard to raise himself. The clouds were gathering more thickly. It began to rain lightly again. Drops of his blood mixed with the rain trickled down the street. Rising, his shoulders bumped up against the cross now hanging over him, the cross casting its shadow across his back. I couldn't reverse my direction quickly enough with the weight of the cross directly over me. Its base wedged itself between two stones in the street. If I pushed back on it, it would begin rising vertically. I felt foolish and awkward in this position. At the same time, a wave of sorrow moved through me for this man. Not even carrying the cross, Jesus struggled to go on.

Unexpectedly, he looked back at me. Almost in a whisper he asked, "Can you go on?"

I nodded my head.

"Simon of Cyrene," he said, "I won't forget what you are doing. This too came to pass, Simon. For both of us, it came to pass."

Close to death, and not even able to stay on his feet, Jesus had still recognized my efforts. Once again, I was no longer some bystander thrown into an unexpected march of torture. How was it that he could see through his pain to me? Did he recognize the grief in my own heart? How could he know? Would my anger and grief pass away? I had no time to think further what he meant.

"Get on your feet now," I pleaded, "or the guards will thrash you again."

He nodded his head slightly and made an effort to get up.

I suddenly felt the sharp sting of a kick in my side from a young soldier out to prove himself in front of his leader, Gustus, whom the young man quickly looked to for approval. He had a broken nose that looked as if it had never been set right. I wanted to break his nose again! Gustus gave him no recognition. My anger quickly subsided. I felt the cross bearing its unforgiving weight on me. I had lost my breath, and I gasped for air as Jesus simply placed his hand where I had been kicked.

No one had heard us, so close were our heads to one another, mine bowed down under the weight of the cross, his coming up from the street. People closest to us began talking among themselves, mocking us. "Are the two planning to rise up against the soldiers and escape? What are they mumbling about to one another? Speak up so we can hear." Their own impatience joined with that of the soldiers. I began to fear we might both be attacked right then. The tension now crackled around us like heat lightning ripping through the darkening clouds.

We stood up together. Those in the crowd lost interest in us as quickly as they had turned on us. A few more, however, had the day free because of the festival and followed us along the narrow way where the soldiers on horseback kept them at a distance. Some people walked along with us for a short while. Others along the street moved in the opposite direction and looked at us for a few moments, as though they had no time for yet another Roman display. At times, the laughter of children playing seemed to get Jesus's attention. He often turned his head in their direction.

Occasionally, I heard the name "Jesus" whispered by one of the common folk in the crowd, a whisper that contained both a certain reverence and a fear that one of the Romans would recognize who had dared call out to him in a sympathetic voice. Who knows what they might do? Jesus tried to see them in the crowd. Not only that, but he seemed comforted by hearing his named called so softly beneath the ridicule and jeering of some. He had friends in the crowd. He had me to help him. He had people on the side of the street trying to give him strength by uttering his name quietly, clearly hoping he would hear them. I watched his bleeding head as it sometimes turned just slightly to the left or right in recognition. He would bow his head in response.

"Let's go. At this rate, we won't get to Golgotha before nightfall," one of the guards complained.

As he carried the burden of his own body in front of me, Jesus seemed more at peace when he heard his name called by those who knew him. On the other hand, he was not disturbed by those people in the festive atmosphere who found him amusing. They stood along the edges of the street or howled down from windows of the buildings nearby. Some even hurled garbage down on the procession and then quickly pulled their heads back so the soldiers could not recognize them. These people knew the Romans would not waste time hunting them down; they were impatient to finish their task.

I saw by the slight turn of his head that Jesus acknowledged these voices by turning toward them. Some mocked him. Others sounded sympathetic and sorrowful themselves. Mostly Jesus bent into himself, keeping his own counsel. In some strange way, when he glanced back at me from time to time, he offered just the slightest hint of recognition. I felt reassured. The cross on my shoulder felt less burdensome, as though his glance had cushioned the place between my shoulder and the hard edge of the cross.

I felt exposed. What if someone recognized me? Someone might think me a follower. In no position to explain, I'd have no defense. This seemed unlikely. And so what? I usually did what was expected of me to gain respectability and a solid position in the community. I would never do anything that would draw attention, bring up questionable motives, or associate me with any but the most established and acceptable business acquaintances and friends. Yes, my respectability was a powerful force that kept me always striving to win approval. This was my legacy from my parents, and this was what I passed to my sons. It was what I had learned and now unlearned.

Here in the street, under the weight of the wood, feeling disapproving eyes on me, I began to think differently. I began to feel even more at ease with the cross I was carrying, with its massive crossbeam cut and beveled to fit into the longer vertical beam that would raise this man into the sky in a short time, now growing more menacing as the day progressed. I could do without the crowd's approval. Could I do without the recognition of this suffering Jesus of Nazareth? I strangely began to feel that I wanted—no, I *needed*—him to understand the terrible grief that kept flaming into angry fire at almost any occasion.

I decided I would keep one eye on the sky, the other on this man in front of me, now moving again, almost without thought or effort, toward his painful death, to see if the storm and this man were meant for each other. Where did I fit in? And what would I do about Albus? How would I find my son Alexander?

Meanwhile, the rain fell lightly on our faces. We kept moving down the narrow increasingly slippery street with Gustus seemingly collapsed in his saddle under the weight of his girth. Barking out orders to his soldiers and me, he drove Jesus ever forward—as if Jesus were a sheep and he was the mocking shepherd.

XIV

Impatiently, a soldier prodded Jesus forward with the end of his spear. More than one soldier shouted for him to hurry up. One pulled out a common wine flask from the pouch of his saddle. He offered a drink to his commander, who waved it off casually, allowing his subordinate to drink and pass the wineskin around. At times, the soldiers would simply lose interest in how the prisoner was doing. Then they would abruptly prod him with their spears, almost as entertainment.

From time to time, the street narrowed. Massive stone archways cast us into momentary darkness. Pushed back against the buildings, the spectators flattened themselves against the walls to let us pass. This caused us to move even more slowly. We had just passed under a low-hanging arch and rounded a corner when a voice suddenly cried out from the crowd, "Jesus! Oh, Jesus, my son. Come to me. Please come to me!"

The soldier with the wine flask immediately charged his horse toward her and got between her and Jesus. "Back woman," he shouted at her. "Get back."

"Jesus," she continued to cry out, and now her voice was mixed with the sounds of her weeping. The soldier seemed shocked by the depth of her pain. He quickly pulled his horse aside.

"It's Mary, his mother," a woman shouted from the crowd.

Not hesitating, Mary shouldered her way through the crowd, aided by three other women. Younger and just as determined, they pushed their way through the crowd to get closer to Jesus. Mary's cry of pain laid down a path before her that even the soldiers hesitated to block.

She made her way to Jesus's side in moments. The crowd grew silent as the soldiers reined in their horses and stopped, staring at the scene before them.

At his side, Mary tenderly wrapped her shawl around Jesus, as though to hide him from the brutality he was enduring. Jesus put one badly bruised arm around her shoulder. For a moment, I thought maybe she could make him disappear within her shawl. Maybe she could somehow reabsorb him into her body and take him away to safety.

The guards, however, seemed momentarily paralyzed. A few soldiers started toward them, stopped, and stepped back. Those on horseback watched intently, and even the horses were strangely quiet. Gustus gave no orders, though several of the soldiers kept looking from Mary and Jesus to him, until he finally said, without much conviction, "Enough. That's enough. Keep moving. Move the prisoner along." But no one seemed eager to separate Mary from her son. Jesus said something to her. Only then did she slowly begin to back away. I could not hear what he said, though she continued to weep. A bewildered look crossed her face.

No one had yet moved.

I had slowly knelt. The massive stone walls on both sides of the street seemed to absorb all but the sounds of Mary's weeping. Down on both knees, I let the crossbeam rest on the wet, slippery stones. The cross creaked noisily at its crossbeams, and the silent crowd and procession could certainly hear it. The crossbeam separated slightly from the vertical beam and created a peculiar angle as I tried to keep it from falling over.

I looked at my own right shoulder. I felt a burning pain. My robe had been torn open by the splinters and roughness of the wood. My shoulder, now swollen, had small lesions where blood oozed and even stained the crux of the cross.

The silence continued except for the wooden end of the cross scraping across the stones in broken sounds as the procession slowly started to move once again. Gustus shouted some orders. The crowd began to talk, muffling the sounds of Mary's loud sobs, which I was anxious to leave behind us. I had the strange thought that the cross was itself groaning in sympathy for Jesus and his mother.

I could only imagine Mary's grief. How could a mother stand the sight of her son suffering so terribly before her very eyes? The sorrow of her son as he had looked at his mother's face through swollen eyes blurred by sweat and blood filled me with anguish as well. What had he said to her? What could he say? Mary's eyes were red and raw from weeping.

How long Mary had been following the procession was hard to say. Perhaps she reached a point where she could no longer stand the sight of her suffering only son and cared nothing for her own safety. This was surely too much for her. She could not have known it would lead to this.

For a few moments while Jesus continued ahead of us, Mary continued to walk alongside me. The guards didn't interfere. I could only surmise that they were relieved to have mother and son separated. She could follow him for a few minutes.

One woman blurted out, "Have you no mothers? Look at her. Look what you're doing to her! For what? What has Jesus done?"

Gustus suddenly rode up and surprisingly addressed the woman while Mary listened intently. "Orders. We have orders. Out of our way. We take no pleasure in this," he said, glancing toward Mary.

Mary put her hands over her face and wept. I did not know what to say. Her sobbing made me feel that I too needed to cry for my loss of Pricilla and Alexander. Amidst the wet smell of the poplar wood and the pungent smell of Jesus, Mary had a fragrance about her as though from another realm. She gave a gentle relief to the smell of the rabble, which was growing more acrid as the air grew heavy with moisture.

Mary's deep feminine presence brought me tearful memories. I recalled the suffering on the face of my son Rufus when he first told me his mother had been killed. I saw once again that terrible grief on his face, mixed with the same anger that I had brought to Jerusalem. How could we bear such a loss?

Seeing Mary's grief for the first time, I began to realize how I was not alone in my grief or my anger. Had my own life not become swollen, bruised, and beaten by my desire for revenge? I had begun to think of myself as a killer who would settle the score with Rome in any way possible, hence ridding myself of the grief I was feeling. Yet how many of the crowd, people like Mary, were also filled with grief and pain? Did I think I was the only one? And what about all the smaller angers and losses that I had felt? Others felt those as well.

Was I not just piling onto my grief every loss I had ever felt? Did my anger not arise from all the ways I had felt thwarted in my life? Now I was so angry I could think only of revenge. Why couldn't I just sob like Mary? The cold steel blade of my knife had edged its way between this weeping mother and me. I didn't know how to sheath it. Yet on Mary's face there had been a distinct contortion of pain as she spoke to her son, so close to him, touching his arm and looking into his face. "My son, my son," she had sobbed softly to him, and I must admit that listening to her made it hard to fight off the anguish in my own heart.

We soon began to pick up the pace. Even Jesus seemed to move more quickly, although he still swayed as he walked forward, and sometimes he even groped ahead of him, as though he found it hard to see. I began to feel relieved as we moved forward. The cross I carried had its own way of keeping people back from us, fearing as they did, perhaps, that they would be contaminated if they even touched the wood I carried on my back. I used it as a barrier for most of the crowd, and it became a guide for others to follow.

Gustus rode up even with me, his thick leg dangling alongside his horse, and shouted, "Get moving. Now. Or it will be your cross as well."

I stopped for a moment, seemingly defying his orders. He placed his hand on the handle of his sword. I then shifted the cross to my left shoulder. As I did, I felt someone gently touch the right side of my face. It was Mary. She had begun to move back into the crowd of people, but she had suddenly reversed her movement. The guards had no time to respond. Still touching my face, she whispered, "Please help him. Help him until the end," she pleaded.

I didn't hesitate. I looked directly into her eyes, and said, "I will. I will do this for him. For you as well."

She nodded her head, turned, and the crowd instantly enveloped her.

When I looked into the deep blueness of her eyes, matched in richness only by the Mediterranean Sea's morning color under a clear sky, I felt reassured, comforted. I could barely stand the look of agony in her face. Her child was about to die. I wanted to seal myself off from her pain. How could I go on and feel her pain? How could I continue marching Jesus toward his death? Did it make sense for me to carry out my own desire to kill and to die as well?

Perhaps Mary knew I would help him. Of course, I had been compelled to help. Those orders became my own at her request. I would do what I could. I felt deeply in myself, and in my shoulders, the weight of what was happening. She had suddenly seemed so young herself, so innocent of all the hatred and foolish fears of Pilate, the crowd, and the stern cruelty of the Romans pushing us forward. What had she done to deserve this? Jesus had gone his own way … and now this. Why? What for?

My moment with her had quickly passed. A foot soldier hurried up behind me, kicked the back of my left leg, and yelled, "Get going! Enough of your stalling. She's not your mother."

I wasn't so sure.

I gripped the cross more firmly, walking more steadily now. I had to see this through. I hardly could have imagined what that would be.

XV

Brooding skies seemed to stretch the morning out. At times, no birds sang. No animals followed the processional in the streets. Some deep gloom had cast itself over the moving parade. In a state that I felt more resembled a dream, the cross began to wear me down. I was tired. Though the clouds covered the sky above, it was still hot.

I slid my right hand over the crossbeam to steady it on my shoulder and felt the sting of a wood sliver pierce my hand. I paused for just a moment to look at it. Blood began to flow. A thin line of blood trickled down my wrist and into the sleeve of my soaked garment. How could such a small piece of wood quickly create such a large aching pain in my palm? Yet I actually welcomed this distraction and was absorbed in what was happening. For a moment, I could forget this march to death, forget Abenadar, Albus, Pilate, and this Jesus of Nazareth. I had a simple pain in my hand to deal with. That was enough.

I began to feel sorry for myself as my clothes grew heavier with perspiration and the light rain turned to a steady drizzle. My legs weakened under the looming burden above and behind me. I felt suffocated by this cross, as if in its own way, it wanted to swallow me, so that I would disappear into its grain and thickness and be absorbed like blood into a sponge. This cross began to feel as if it had a life of its own. It and the man in front of me, shuffling in bare feet, having to feel the pain of the uneven stones against the bottoms of his feet, now seemed to be in a strange conspiracy with me. I was an unwilling accomplice. For a moment, I imagined the cross growing branches and enveloping me in its leafy arms, where I could hide and maybe even escape.

The sliver in my hand settled down to a dull ache. My flesh seemed to absorb it with less throbbing than I'd felt when it drilled itself into me. Keep going at all costs, I convinced myself. I looked at the crowd. I saw the curious straining to get a glimpse of the beaten prisoner. Others were indifferent to Jesus and hardly glanced our way. A few had looks of horror on their faces. Some were angry, shouting indiscriminately at the guards and Jesus. I looked at the buildings made of massive stone blocks, which were unevenly placed, many looking as if they might fall out of place at any time, bringing buildings tumbling down on us. I imagined the entire city collapsing in rubble around us all.

Occasionally, gracefully designed archways smoothed the sharp edges of most of the massive square stone walls of the buildings on each side of us. The roughly placed uneven stones of the street relieved some of the monotony of the journey, or at least diverted me from the grief squeezing my heart. They had become obstacles to any smooth movement down the street. I knew that I could easily trip and fall in an instant, and I would suddenly be pinned by the weight of the cross.

"Keep it moving!" Gustus shouted at us. Another soldier cracked a whip over my head. Another pushed Jesus forward. A few began to argue with one other, and one cursed the rain that had now made the street even more slippery and dangerous to walk on.

"Shut it up!" Gustus ordered. His soldiers obeyed.

I now gripped the cross more firmly, as though seeking protection from the guards' increasingly hostile voices. Perhaps they had begun to rehearse for Golgotha by already calling up their hardness toward us. Their horses must have sensed the tension, for they skittishly began butting into the crowd, which quickly drew back.

One old man, hit hard by the chest of a horse, fell to the ground and cracked his head on the stones. A few rushed to help him. The soldiers held them back. The man writhed on the street and appeared unable to get up. He was forced to crawl into the crowd, where he collapsed, while the guards laughed at his undignified exit. Many began to shout at the soldiers, and the soldiers yelled back.

Gustus again intervened, shouting at his men. The soldiers pulled back, but the crowd kept shouting their insults. The rain lessened. The crowd began to grow quiet as we continued to move forward slowly.

Before long, the procession slowed again as we approached a difficult place for the horses. The soldiers dismounted and began to lead them.

I had to pay close attention as we entered a part of the street where the steps were placed several feet apart, making it difficult for the horses to descend. I tried to prepare for the descent and for the foot of the cross to drop from one step to the next. Reverberations pained my shoulder as they went from the base up the vertical beam to where the crossbeam intersected with it. Right in that crux was my shoulder. I could not soften the blows. My despair and fatigue grew from just the thought of what was to come from the cross dropping across the stones. I tried not to think too much ahead of what was happening.

A painful voice interrupted my worry. "I know him," a young woman's voice cried out. Her assertion sounded over the chatter of the crowd. A young woman in modest clothing, black except for a brown head covering, and carrying a white cloth about the size of a woman's shawl, squeezed along the wall. She pushed her way through the crowd and walked quickly to Jesus. The guards were surprised, reacting slowly.

Warning her, someone called out her name, "Veronica! Stay away. Come back!"

She paid them no heed. In an instant, she stood next to Jesus. Surprisingly, the guards used this intrusion, rather than as an excuse to thrash her, as a way to bring the procession to a temporary halt before descending the steps. In the narrow passage, the guards had difficultly dismounting, and they clearly welcomed the interruption. They could now rest for a few moments and at the same time calm their horses, now restless in the steep passageway.

The guard with the wine flask began passing it to the foot soldier. Several other soldiers, including Gustus, leaned against the stone buildings to rest as well. Their uniforms were blazoned and intimidating, their helmets heavy, which made their heads sweat profusely in the sultry air that grew dense with moisture and the stagnant smell of the city. A few removed their helmets and held them at their sides;

their faces revealed their youthfulness. Helmets off, they seemed so harmless.

I knew better. I would always know better. That's how Albus had looked. He had looked like one of them. He stood there, a youthful soldier, about the age of my sons, at our well, with helmet in hand, obedient to Abenadar and to his lustful orders. Albus had killed Pricilla. There was no forgetting that.

I lowered the cross to find some relief. Jesus had looked up at the woman called Veronica. Jesus's long hair had fallen randomly across his face. His hair dripped with sweat and blood, forming droplets of pink liquid before sliding off the ends of his tangled strands. His beard was soaked with sweat and dirt, directing blood down the rivulets of his face. He had turned toward Veronica and seemed puzzled by her approach. She had simply stopped the entire forward movement of the procession with her boldness. Now she stood next to him, and the eyes of the crowd and the soldiers were all on her.

Veronica's youthful beauty did not go unnoticed by the guards. They made remarks about her, laughing in her direction as she spoke to Jesus in a whisper. For a moment, the rage began to take hold of me again. I tried to concentrate on Veronica, which lessened my rush of anger. I could not hear her words. I saw only the anguish in her face, which matched his. Their suffering mirrored each other's as she revealed the deepening horror of Jesus's pain.

To our surprise, Veronica grasped her shawl and began tenderly, starting in one small corner of Jesus's face, to wipe the blood, sweat, and dirt from it. Jesus lifted his head slightly to meet her gentle touch. The crowd watched as though transfixed by her simple act. The guards seemed puzzled about what to do.

"What right has she?" I heard someone in the crowd shout. "Get her out of there."

Veronica softly and deftly held the back of Jesus's neck to steady his face against the pressure of the cloth. She wiped his forehead, taking great care not to let the cloth snag in any of the sharp thorns sticking straight out of the wreath that encircled his head.

A young woman, Veronica moved with the confidence and grace of a regal Jewess. She had large eyes, a sharply chiseled nose, and long black hair. Something about her reminded me of Pricilla. I thought of the many times I had followed Pricilla's own dark hair from her navel down into her moist opening. I was puzzled by my sudden desire. Was I so different from these lustful young soldiers? Didn't I desire Veronica as well? I knew it wasn't her, though. It could have been just about any woman. Unlike my love for Pricilla, I just wanted Veronica, or some woman, to take me out of the horrible grief and anger that were buried in the cross I was carrying. I'd confused lust with my desire to be mothered out of my situation. My desire seemed so foolish. I realized I wanted some of the very tenderness she was giving to Jesus. What did I think Veronica was? Some bottomless goblet of wine?

Veronica looked at Jesus with what appeared to be sincere compassion. Her hand seemed to be guided by an invisible force as she washed both sides of his face. Shaking the cloth for a moment, finding a clean place on it, she gathered it around and under his beard with both hands, wiping with downward strokes to remove the dirt and blood that now mingled on the cloth. Immediately, the effects of her tenderness appeared on the Nazarene's face. Jesus looked younger, as if her wiping his face had restored his youthfulness and had revealed a beauty hidden beneath all the hatred that had been strewn across it.

I suddenly felt uneasy. The horses became skittish. One of them began to rear up, neighing loudly, while a soldier turned around and pulled hard at its knotted reins. When the horse settled, I noticed for the first time the silence that had spread across all the people. If I closed my eyes, which I did for an instant, the throng around us seemed to disappear. It was as if the Romans had given an order for everyone to cease breathing and they had obeyed.

I opened my eyes and scanned the crowd. My gaze came to rest on Veronica, who was standing just about the length of the cross in front of me. In her hand, she held the cloth that she had been using to wipe Jesus's face. It was slack in her left hand, which was held out exactly in front of her, as if waiting for someone to run by and snap it from her. Her other hand covered her mouth. Her eyes had widened. Her breath came in short gasps, her chest moving rapidly, like an athlete who had been sprinting through the races at the festival. Not moving, she stood staring at the cloth as she slowly and carefully, as if trying to untie a spider's web, opened the cloth. That's when the back of her hand went to her mouth. A perfectly reflected image of Jesus appeared on the cloth! I looked at Jesus. I then looked at the cloth. The image was of Jesus—*before* she had wiped his face!

He looked serene, as if asleep in a tranquil pose of death. A slight smile played on his face, like one dreaming some pleasant and satisfying scene. The past had been captured in the present—his visage permanently stained into the present and soaked into the cloth. A few others close to Veronica, pressed against the wall in the narrow passageway, gave a collective gasp. The soldiers standing close by seemed utterly confused.

I didn't know what to think. I could only wonder with the rest of the crowd what had occurred. Veronica, having taken the cloth with both hands, held it up, as if to dry it in the moist breeze blowing through the street. We could see it clearly. Those lining the streets huddled closer to each other. A few covered their faces and refused to look.

"He's the devil himself!" an old man shouted, breaking the silence. He waved his cane menacingly at the Nazarene. "Kill him now. He's possessed."

"He serves the devil. I know it," answered his companion, a wizened old fellow.

"No, this is just like him!" cried out a woman. "I saw him do something like this once before." The crowed turned to hear her out.

Those of us close to the woman listened with half attention to her story. She was telling how Jesus had healed people on the Sabbath. He had done strange things to people who were sick. He had driven evil spirits out of them, directing them into swine, and driven them over a cliff. A few began to listen more closely to her. We, however, were more interested in peering closely at the cloth, which was quivering a bit, small ripples moving through it in quick succession, like a flag of flesh!

Veronica appeared nervous as some in the crowd started to make their way into the street to get closer to her, straining to get a look. The soldiers, transfixed by the image that had materialized on the cloth, were nonetheless quick to push the crowd back quickly, surely fearing an entire breakdown of the procession.

Meanwhile, Jesus serenely surveyed the crowd. He was clearly puzzled by our reactions. It was as though nothing out of the ordinary had happened. He looked with bewilderment on our confusion and fear.

Veronica's tenderness had surprisingly affected me. What was I to make of this?

A few women knelt down on the wet, hard stones and began to pray as the rain suddenly let up. Others bolted from the crowd and headed down alleyways close by, either in fright or to fetch friends to see this cloth before it disappeared or was confiscated by the Romans and destroyed on the spot. It seemed a kind of evidence of something. Some clear sign of another law?

Veronica, now shaking her head as if from a deep trance, carefully wrapped up the cloth. She tucked it into the folds of her own garments, as if sensing that something could happen to it now, especially from the Roman officers and soldiers.

After lightly kissing Jesus's brow, she turned and disappeared into the crowd. Gustus shouted at us. Carefully, a step at a time, I descended the stairs, the foot of the cross bumping along behind me. None of us quite understood what had happened, and it would not be the only time Jesus confounded our usual expectations.

XVI

I made my way down the steps slowly and carefully. It was as if I had just awakened from a dream. Moments ago, sounds had ceased, and the pain of carrying the cross had subsided. But now, slowly, the shouting, the wetness of the street, the clouds thickening and hanging overhead, the Roman soldiers' horses snorting, and the foot soldiers once again pushing back the crowd came drifting back into my awareness. Perhaps it was only in some dream state that I had called Jesus "master." Wasn't it the present circumstances coming back to me now?

Clearly anxious to make up the time, the guards pushed and prodded Jesus with their spears. Piercing his back, one guard caused a dark bloodstain to begin forming on his dirty clothing. It slowly but evenly spread out in a narrow line, like a small waterfall, soaking through the worn gray cloth. He was being prodded to move ever faster, like an animal cruelly driven before an insensitive master. Jesus took a few hurried steps and fell again.

"Not so rough, you fool. We'll be taking a dead body to Golgotha!" shouted one of the guards. And with those words, his whip came down hard on the young soldier, just missing Jesus's face. The young man instinctively cowered under the lash. It cracked harmlessly against his helmet.

The soldier's display of his whip reminded me of how pathetically Albus had been treated by Abenadar at our well. They seemed locked into their little game of power, Albus playing the victim and the other providing the cruelty. And then, in a sudden reversal of roles, Albus slit my wife's throat. The brutal game had finally resulted in her death. I intended to soon end their game once and for all.

The spears periodically driven into Jesus's back had weakened him even further. The black spot on the back of his clothing spread out slowly, as olive oil will do when a jug is suddenly spilled. As the caravan continued forward, I was unable to look away from the blood soaking the cloth on his back. How did he keep moving forward with such erratic steps?

We soon turned into another street leading toward the city walls and then to the end of this poor man's suffering. Not that far away Golgotha, the place of a skull, awaited Jesus. I felt a moment of relief that soon this might all be over. I could still carry out my own plans and be free from the agony of this march.

The procession moved slowly. Although no longer sure of how much time had passed, I knew it had been hours. So many steps taken, one after another, the cross driving me down into the hard stones of the streets, step by step. It seemed we would never reach the end, and I began to resent any interruptions. Although I probably had not walked long with the cross, I felt dizzy and now used it to steady myself. I thought I too could easily collapse at some point.

The crowd had thinned out, perhaps because some had lost interest, while others may have tired from the numerous stops we had made. Some may have walked on ahead to Golgotha to wait for the execution party to arrive. I heard that during previous executions, some would bring food, spread out a lamb's skin on the ground, and wait for the entertainment of the howls of pain coming from those being crucified.

I shifted the weight of the cross to my left shoulder and felt it groan when I not so much lifted it as slid myself from one side to the other. I had become quite adept at this by this time. I worked with the cross's weight instead of fighting it to give myself a break from its relentless companionship. I had learned to slide my body under it with a kind of dexterity that relieved me of so much effort. It slipped along better as the stones remained moist, for the sky had poured several hard rains on us.

I wished someone could further wet the street in front of me so that the weight of the cross could be lessened even more. I found I was looking for ways to make carrying this burden easier, and I felt a tinge of shame for it. This would finally be his cross, not mine. Soon the roles would be reversed. This cross would bear the burden of Jesus's exhausted body, and on it, he would come to his final end.

My suffering, I knew, was temporary, meager, compared to the imminent suffering Jesus would have to endure. Just then, he glanced back at me. He slightly nodded his head at me, and I knew that he saw my own struggle. Following him so closely, I knew he could easily be reminded of the cross he would soon die upon. I hoped he might see me and not only the cross. I wanted to hide the brutal reminder. Its loud scraping across the stones began to unsettle me even more than his look. Did he hear the cross being dragged along behind him, following him, haunting him as he walked forward to his death?

My musings were brought to an abrupt halt. A soldier cried out, "You, Jew! Stop!"

Jesus had fallen once again. He hit his face against the stone street, only partially breaking his fall with his shoulder. The crowd gasped. He lay motionless for an instant before he turned his head a bit. How could he possibly make it to his place of execution? My hope that I could make this journey easier suddenly abandoned me. The little hope I had clung to now suddenly collapsed inside me like a tent whose poles had just been kicked out from under it. I was stunned by his sudden fall.

The same soldier barked orders at me again. "You, Jew. Help him up. And you," pointing to a young man, "hold the cross for him."

The youth, hardly fifteen years of age, wearing clothing of dark red and white, half stepped forward before his giggling companions pushed him the rest of the way. He walked out from the crowd and took his place next to me, obviously embarrassed by this sudden attention.

"Here," I said to him, looking into his face, "just balance this cross on its beam. Don't let it fall."

The boy nodded to me. He uttered a subdued, "Why do I have to?" I heard something in his voice that sounded familiar and strange at the same time. I looked more closely at him. I noticed with some pleasure how much he looked like my son Alexander when he was a young boy. Ask Alexander to help in the barn, and the words could be his as well: "Why do I have to?"

Oh, how I missed my son. Somehow, I had to find him as well. It was not enough to avenge Pricilla. I wanted my son back.

The young boy held the cross upright with a steady hand. Freed from its burden and from its responsibility for the first time since I had shouldered it and lifted it from the ground, I hurried to Jesus. Painfully moving his body from side to side, he couldn't get up.

"Get him up. Be quick about it," one of the guards on horseback ordered me. To prove his point, he brought his horse right up to Jesus and me. I smelled his leathery, sweaty body and the aroma of the horse that always made me feel at peace as a youth. But this horse, a beautiful and muscular Arabian—dark, inky, and as shiny as the wet skin of a black olive—stomped around us in menacing skittish turns. His left rear hoof almost came down on Jesus's right leg as he lifted himself on all fours in a desperate effort to raise himself. I feared we both might be trampled.

Watching Jesus lying there so helpless, I wished he would not get up. I felt a dark cloud of despair and hopelessness. He wouldn't make it to the end. Neither would I. I had to escape. I still had my revenge locked inside. Even the young man who was now helping me reminded me of Albus. There was no going back on the promises I had made to Pricilla and my son. This Jesus seemed to be diverting me from my task, but that wouldn't be for long. If I could escape, I could go look for Albus and free myself from the ugly parade of death that had begun with Pricilla's death.

I looked from Jesus to the young man now balancing the cross with dexterity and a little bravado. If I were to walk backward into the crowd while all eyes were on the fallen Jesus or the young man balancing the cross in a demonstration of agility for the crowd, I could escape this tyranny. I could run down the narrow alley. I could lose any pursuers in the labyrinth of the city.

I took a few steps backward, and then my moment of escape quickly passed. "If this horse steps on you, Nazarene, don't blame me," one of the soldiers said, laughing and glancing at Gustus, who was watching the exchange. Jesus's eyes were barely open. He turned his head to look at me and then turned away again.

I slowly lifted him to his feet. I felt a sudden stabbing pain in my forehead as I got him up. One of the thorns on the back of Jesus's head had stabbed me like a small spear—right in the middle of my forehead. The thorn broke off midpoint. I winced in pain and let out a slight cry.

Jesus saw the broken thorn sticking out from my forehead. Quickly, he reached over and pulled it out. He pressed the thorn into my open palm. I closed my fingers around it and then deftly tucked it into my robe. I released him, feeling in his body that he could now stand by himself. I was astonished by what I suddenly said to him: "Master, we must go on." He nodded his head, sighed deeply, turned, and once again began to stagger forward.

Master? I had not planned to say that, to address him that way. I had whispered it, but I'd heard myself, and I could see that Jesus had too. It did not seem to strike him as surprising. His face remained calm, even serene, and a little distant. But I did not understand why I had said that. Why would I call him master? What was he mastering? Hardly in charge of anything, including his own body, Jesus looked more like a slave serving the cruel brutality of Rome's intention to keep order in Jerusalem—no matter what the cost. No matter what, his death was inevitable. There was no way out for him. Only by following him to the end would I get out of this alive and be free to avenge the death of my wife. I had to see this through, not just for him, not just for his mother, Mary. No. For me as well. Yes, for Jesus as well. Who says I can't have more than one reason for my actions?

XVII

I took the cross from the young man. He kept one hand on the crossbeam, as though reluctant to let it go, and I simply said to him, "Well done, my friend."

"What's he done to be crucified?" he suddenly asked.

"He said he was king of the Jews," I told him.

"Is he?" the young man responded.

"Some say he is," I replied. "Others say he is a traitor, loyal to some other kingdom. Others say he is the Messiah, the son of God. Who knows? I'm not sure what he said. He doesn't make a lot of claims for himself."

"Did his face come off on some woman's cloth?" he asked.

"I saw the shape of his face appear there. It looked like his face before she wiped it."

"What happened next?" he asked.

"She ran off with the cloth," I said. "She didn't want the Romans to get it. They'd use it against Jesus's followers."

Our brief conversation was abruptly interrupted. "Let's go … and now!" a guard yelled. I quickly began to move forward. The young boy started to follow me.

"Can I come?" he asked.

"What's your name?" I asked.

"James" he said.

"Why not? Come along, James," I replied. "The guards don't seem to care. They probably think I may need you. And I might."

Even after the brief rest, the cross felt heavier now. I also felt a bit comforted by its familiarity, not feeling complete without it. But the guards noticed now that James was walking beside me and behind Jesus. One guard came over with a whip, snapping it above James's head, forcing him suddenly back into the crowd. I glanced at him, and our eyes met. He half lifted his arm to wave at me, and as I turned and continued, I felt more alone now. I wondered if I'd ever see James again.

My thoughts turned to Rufus. Had he found out anything about Alexander? I wished he were here. I wanted him to tell me what he knew. Surely someone knew something about whom the Romans were holding, and why. If anyone could find out, I knew Rufus would.

As soon as I thought of Rufus, I thought about Pricilla. I could not avoid thinking of her being killed by Albus. Looking at the blood on the back of Jesus's robe, I envisioned the blood flowing out of the mouth of Albus and over the face of my wife, and Jesus and Albus and my wife suddenly seemed to mingle before me. My one free hand instinctively reached under my robe and felt for my knife. It was still there. I had not touched it for some time now. I felt reassured. No guard had thought to search me. I still had my knife. Once again, my hatred for Albus began to strengthen my resolve.

Three Romans on horses were now leading the procession, followed by three soldiers on foot, with Gustus asserting his command from time to time, his orders sounding random at best. He seemed to like the sound of his own shrill voice. Jesus and I followed, with about a dozen people also walking behind us, as if they had made themselves part of the official caravan to Golgotha. All trudged forward, turning down a length of the road that looked more like an alley than a street. Only a few handfuls of people were present, seeming slightly curious about the prisoner. Then we were on to the main street, where more of the crowd had gathered. This road would soon carry us all outside the walls of Jerusalem.

I noticed that the atmosphere on this street was different. Coming into view was a group of women all dressed in black. They advanced toward us. They wore black shawls on their heads, and they clustered close together, amplifying a melodic sound of wailing. As the sorrowful caravan approached us, Jesus slowed his already slow pace.

The procession barely moved forward, much to the annoyance of the impatient guards.

A low moaning rose up from the women, sounding like cattle together in the pasture, especially after their young calves were separated from them and put into a field some distance from their mothers. It was a combination of wailing and chanting, with its own rhythms, rising and falling, rising and falling. As we approached, I felt we were entering something like a series of waves on the sea. Their sounds, not words exactly, in their rhythmic rising and falling, mixed with the constant sound of the cross being dragged, sometimes bumping across the uneven stones.

Enacting a long tradition in Jerusalem, these noble women of the city would stand by the roadside or the street and offer some refreshing drink—plain water or water mixed with wine—to the condemned. Not the wine commonly carried by guards, mixed with gall that could numb the pain of a prisoner, their wine nevertheless helped make the criminals' last hours on Earth a bit more humane, made them feel they were not alone. The Romans or Jewish leaders posted notices regarding the condemned in the city square. From the postings, the women knew about most executions. They would then meet some place on the road, in a group, to offer prisoners libations. Jesus was to be no exception. Obligated to accept their presence, the Roman soldiers yielded for a moment to their kindness, and some drank themselves, though visibly resentful at the interference.

One old woman stepped forward. The wrinkles on her face seemed to be drawn straight down to her lips, and she spoke out of the corner of her mouth. "This wine is for you, Jesus of Nazareth," she said softly. Her hand trembled as she lifted the cup to his lips.

Jesus took the cup. He thanked her, while looking at her and the other women behind her, about nine in number.

I had gradually moved closer to Jesus. The guards hardly seemed to notice. I could hear Jesus speak to the women. "You, too, are my disciples," he said to them. "For you have stayed with me in my darkest hour." He sipped the wine slowly. I stopped behind Jesus and crouched down under the cross to unburden myself. Jesus slowly backed away from the women. With the cup of wine now half-full, he turned, and offered the remaining to me. Surprised at his unexpected gesture of kindness, I reluctantly took the goblet of wine and took a small sip. He needed the wine much more than I did. Or was he telling me something else? For an instant, I had the crazy thought that I wanted to give him back my knife in return. I regained my sense. If I reached for my knife near him, the nearest guard would instantly kill me. I carefully felt for it. It was still in place.

"Master, you finish it," I said to him, handing it back and shifting the cross to my other shoulder. I tried to look as if the cross were not so burdensome. Actually, I was feeling dizzy and nauseous from its weight, and I wished to simply drop it. I wanted to cut it away from me forever. It had become like a diseased limb or growth that made my own body feel unnatural and even unruly.

Jesus did not speak to me. He came over and held the cup—a rich gold one, with tiny jewels embedded in its base—near my lips. I could not refuse. I reluctantly took it and drank deeply. I handed it back to him with a nod of gratitude. When I returned it to him, I noticed with some concern that my hands were rather shaky, as if I had palsy or some malady that was beginning to affect me. I felt both my strength and my weakness at this moment. Jesus smiled faintly at me. "Simon," he said, looking directly at me, "you seem sorely troubled. I will pray you will live again."

I could hardly look at him, and I immediately lowered my eyes, stunned by what he had said. What did he know about my troubles? Anything? My grief? The anger that burned in me? Who asked for his prayers? The warmth of the wine spread through my body, drowning my questions. I could think of nothing to say. When I raised my head, I saw he had turned away, giving the cup back to the old woman with the shriveled face.

The group of women continued to mourn loudly for him. He turned and addressed them. "Daughters of Jerusalem, do not weep for me. Weep rather for yourselves and for your children…"

Unexpectedly, and I'm sure I can speak for the others as well, those of us who thought we were helping Jesus became the ones in need of help. That went for our children as well. No wonder I didn't want his prayers. I didn't want help. Jesus wasn't the only one who needed help. We all did. Jesus, once again, seemed to be drawing us into some common sorrow in our world. I wanted no part of it.

The wine, though, had somewhat revived me from my fatigue. The warmth from it seemed to push me away from death's door. The wind picked up slightly, and I turned my face into it, feeling refreshed. The darkening clouds hung lower over the city now, carrying the promise of heavy rain. I had grown somewhat accustomed to my station in this procession, following the footsteps and the pace of the wounded Nazarene.

There seemed to be less rancor among the crowd and among those who now followed the procession. Those who had been swilling wine or calling for the one who claimed to be able to destroy the temple and to build it up again in three days' time—a preposterous proposition by any standards, they argued—were either gone or had quieted their anger.

"Cyrenean," I heard a voice call out. "It's me, James!"

I turned to see the young man who had briefly helped me with the cross. He was making his way along the edge of the crowd. How did he know where I was from, and why did he keep following along? A few guards noted his eager attention to the cross and me, and I feared he might be in danger. I signaled to him to go away, and I saw him drop his head and blend back into the crowd.

The crowd now following was plainly fascinated by Jesus. Others had lost interest or simply watched as the procession passed them by. Those who now followed seemed more a part of the procession. It was as though they belonged, more drawn into what they had not expected at first. What were they seeing in this man called Jesus? About thirty or so people, the people who now seemed more sympathetic to the prisoner stumbling, fell in line behind me and the soldiers at my back.

I turned occasionally to see the guards looking nervously behind themselves. Gustus often shouted for them to keep Jesus moving, although it was clear he was moving as fast as he could, and Gustus's commands were simply swept away by the wind. Gustus moved two of the soldiers from the front of the procession and placed them between himself and the crowd that followed.

Jesus's words came drifting back to me. He'd pray for me. So I could live. Something like that.

So I could live? Live for what? For my dead wife and lost son? What did he know about living?

XVIII

A loud commotion arose on a side street. Gustus ordered us to stop. The crowd suddenly parted to my left and slightly behind me. I put the cross down and turned to see what was happening. From down the side street, three Roman guards with long spears pushed two dirty and beaten criminals. They constantly prodded one of the prisoners with the ends of their spears. Another soldier on horseback was clearly in charge, shouting orders to his foot soldiers, ordering them to move faster.

One prisoner kept turning and cursing the guards. Every time he did, the soldiers would give him a shove and prod him with a spear. He had long stringy hair, was missing a few of his front teeth and was thin, like a donkey that had been neglected. His rib cage stuck out so you could count his exposed bones.

"Ah, the comrade of Barabbas," I heard someone in the crowd announce. "He's not one of the prisoners released today from the synagogues. Too bad for him."

"How could the crowd choose Barabbas over Jesus?" someone asked.

There was no answer. And now these two criminals were destined for crucifixion alongside Jesus.

Gustus acknowledged the leader of the group just joining us, and he saluted Gustus, deferring to his command. Quickly, the guards and the two prisoners fell in line not too far behind me. Mostly grateful for the small break in our march, I gave them scant attention. The guards were eager to keep us moving, and it was hard to sort out the prisoner's defiant remarks from the guards' orders, and sometimes the commands of one foot soldier seemed particularly difficult to understand. I tried to shut out what they were saying. Before long, they started to lag further behind me. On occasion, their leader would ride up on his horse, circle the prisoners, and then return to his place behind them.

It would be a busy afternoon. I understood now better than before why the guards kept trying to move us along. They had three prisoners to execute at once. Death would not pass them over. I closed my eyes in anticipation of what was ahead, already beginning to plan how I would simply disappear into the crowd once I had delivered the cross to its destination. I did not want to witness the carnage that would soon be strewn across the place of skulls.

Occasionally, I glanced back at the two criminals, hardly noticing the soldiers. The younger criminal looked much healthier, fuller, and certainly more muscular than the other. Neither had shirts. Both showed bruises on their faces, chests, and legs. I could not see their backs. The younger man, if washed and dressed, could look like one of my own sons: respectable, even handsome, and from a good family. What had he done, I wondered, to expose himself to crucifixion at such a young age? He could not be more than twenty or so. But here he was, following along behind Jesus and me.

"Look at this, now, will you?" said the older criminal to the younger. "We're in a parade." He surveyed the crowd and spat a huge wad from his mouth, hitting an older woman in the face. Without hesitating, she spat back at him, and he ducked and laughed.

A guard intervened. "Walk ahead of your friend," he ordered the younger man.

"He's not my friend," answered the younger fellow, certainly not wanting to be beaten like the older and increasingly defiant criminal.

The younger prisoner moved faster, and to my surprise, he began walking alongside me. He tried to strike up a conversation, "What have you done?" he asked me.

"I've done nothing," I told him. "I was ordered by the Romans to carry this cross to Golgotha. Then I'm free to go. And you, why are you condemned?"

"I killed a man in an argument … killed him with a large stone after he tried to rob me," he replied.

I suddenly felt a shudder go through my body. He looked so innocent. He had sought to defend himself. And what about me? Hadn't I sought to kill Pilate? What was the difference between this man and me? He had been caught. I hadn't had the chance to kill. Not yet.

The criminal went on. "The man I killed was a drunk. He tried to rob me. Turns out he was related to one of the centurions from Rome. He was in the wrong, robbing me, but he had connections. I didn't control my anger. So today I die."

I could see the terror but also the resignation in his face. Then he added, "I know that man ahead of you. He preached in Judea for some time. I used to follow and listen to him. I liked his simple sayings, one in particular: when he spoke of himself as a vine and those of us listening as offshoots of it. The vine, he said, is the source of life."

"You call this life?" I asked.

He didn't answer that, and I wished I hadn't questioned him. He continued.

"It is unbelievable that I am following him now to his death. I really did not think I would ever see him again. I lost track of where he and his disciples were heading. I didn't think he would come into Jerusalem for the Passover festival. But now it makes sense that this is where he would want to be."

"It doesn't make much sense to me," I replied. "Look what it's gotten him. This cross."

A look of fear crossed the young man's face, and he slowed his pace and fell behind me now.

Jesus's pace increased a bit. I settled under the cross and shouldered it with a bit more energy, dragging it, listening to its varied sounds across the stones, wood playing on stone, clunking over some of the more uneven ones. I did not want to fall now. I looked at the growing size of outcasts, including myself, a mere stranger from Cyrene. So many years, an entire life, I thought, of being within the established, respectable order. But today, in an instant, I was thrown into the darkness of death and suffering. I had become an outsider, an exile, looked down upon by most of the people lining the street.

This young man, who had dropped behind me but in front of his cursing criminal partner, avoiding the latter and the crowd's jeers and hollering by staring straight ahead, brought me back to my son Alexander. I thought of the terror I would feel if I were along the buildings as a spectator, and suddenly saw my oldest son in such a procession, hands tied with rope, stripped to nothing but the cloth covering his loins, barefoot, being taken out to Golgotha as a common criminal and crucified. A fear passed through me that maybe Rome had found some excuse to crucify Alexander. It was possible. Where had they taken him? Maybe he had seen too much, knew too much, and they planned to get rid of him.

No, I would not be able to live with that. I would plead with the guards to let me go in his place. "Please," I would beg, stepping into the street, unafraid of their whips, spears, swords, and furious and beautiful horses. "Please let me replace this youth. He is my son. I cannot stand by. Take me instead." It would be easier for me to feel the pain and humiliation of crucifixion myself than to stand by and witness my son executed. I would plead, "Let me go in his place. Don't execute him. Take me."

Then I imagined the guard saying, "No, crazy man. Step back out of the street or I'll call for the guards to arrest you. You can spend some months in prison to get over your desire to die instead of your son. Now get back." I imagined his horse, with its beautiful animal smell and gallant chest, coming directly at me, pushing me back into the crowd.

All of what was taking place around me as we slowed our pace toward Golgotha incited sweet and painful memories of raising my sons, worrying about them every day—that they would fall prey to the disasters that were part of our lives. I felt the anguish of knowing how Pricilla might have felt the moment before she died, suddenly torn apart in her body and torn away from her sons ... and me as well.

All these thoughts—the man in front of me being led to his death, the young man also condemned, myself between them—brought tears to my eyes. I hung my head under the cross and pretended to be shouldering the wood with more determination. I could hardly bear what was happening to me now. I was suddenly filled once again with a deep, unspeakable sorrow. I wanted to cry out for my wife and son Alexander. I thought I was losing my mind. How could this be me? It was a stranger inside of me trying to puncture my skin and find air to breathe, while

I struggled with this cross as if carrying it now meant something more than following an order.

Suddenly, there was the crack of a whip just above my head, abruptly ending my reverie. A soldier had moved a few feet from me. It was as though cold water had been thrown in my face. A surge of anger welled up in me as I turned toward the guard. He uttered something I could not understand. His commander quickly rode up to us and began talking to the foot soldier. I only glanced their way.

The glance was enough. Instantly, I saw the long scar on the horseman's face. It cut across his left eyebrow. It was Abenadar!

I couldn't believe my eyes. I quickly looked at the soldier he was addressing. The soldier on foot was mumbling something unclear to Abenadar. Abenadar was leaning toward him from his saddle, trying to make sense of what he was saying. The soldier's tongue darted strangely in and out of his mouth. I saw with pleasure how it had been mutilated, torn apart on one side.

It was Albus, the nearly tongueless bastard! He was one of those guarding the other two prisoners. Abenadar was still his commander in charge of getting the two new prisoners to their crucifixion. Albus would go to Golgotha. There, I would crush his skull into the hill with all the other skulls. If I could, I would get Abenadar as well.

Gustus suddenly rode up. "What's the trouble?" he asked Abenadar. "No trouble at all," Abenadar replied, his voice slightly subservient.

"Then let's move on," commanded Gustus.

"As you will," replied Abenadar, who turned in his saddle and seemed to give me a long look.

I quickly turned my head. I don't think he had recognized me. Albus hadn't looked my way. They had hardly seen me. I calmed myself and felt my fear subside. They had no reason to expect to see me ever again, least of all in this place. A month had passed. He'd hardly remember me, especially with all the men intent on their tasks. I was just a person pulled out of the streets to carry the cross of Jesus. I was simply one part of a parade to Golgotha ... with a minor role to fulfill.

Albus had only seen that I had slowed my pace. They couldn't care less whom they cracked a whip over. I grasped the cross more firmly and moved forward. I wanted gradually, without calling attention to myself, to put some distance between us. Yet Albus and the two prisoners stayed close behind. Having Albus close to me would be to my advantage when the time came for me to turn on him. I could still hear Abenadar and Albus talk as they ordered the prisoners to move faster, having incurred the displeasure of Gustus, who seemed to be more and more impatient with us all.

I would make sure not to get in their way. I wouldn't slow their pace. I wouldn't call attention to myself. Under the cross, with my head down toward the ground and turned slightly, I could easily see Albus walking closely behind the prisoners, taking turns prodding them, though I was surprised at Albus's seeming lack of irritation with the prisoners whenever Abenadar was distracted by the crowd. I'd expected him to be more hardened. Apparently now satisfied with my pace, Albus was concentrating entirely on his two prisoners while Abenadar pulled his horse back in line to ride alongside Gustus, who was clearly in charge of the entire procession.

I instinctively felt for my knife. It was there, in place. Albus and Abenadar following along with me! Albus on foot. Not far behind me. Now it was a matter of time. My time. The right time. I could not believe my good fortune.

Looking ahead toward Jesus, I realized that he had turned to look at me. I lowered my eyes and looked away from him. Strangely, my spirits lifted. Some new strength enabled me to move forward. As though it had finally found its place, Jesus's cross was nestled firmly on my shoulder. Now it felt lighter than it had moments before. It was a burden I'd soon shed. When I did, I would be free to follow the lead of my knife across the neck of Albus. I'd have my chance. This might all be easier than I'd thought. I would have my revenge. I could at least kill Albus. I might even escape if I waited for the right moment.

XIX

As I moved forward with the cross, I suddenly realized how strange this all had become. It was as though Albus, the object of my hatred, the source of my endless grief and anger, pressed me from behind. He carried with him the blood of Pricilla and the ache of Alexander, my lost son. And yet, not far ahead, this Jesus of Nazareth, whom I'd heard so much about, seemed to be calling me forward with him toward his certain end. How could it be that I was now caught between the horror of my past, stuffed into the person called Albus and a strange unknown person called Jesus, who was taking the very worst that all of us, including the Roman Empire, could heap upon him?

How did I end up carrying another person's cross between Albus and Jesus? While I continued to catch glimpses of Albus behind me and heard him struggling to speak, there was no question that for now I had to move forward. That meant I had to follow this Nazarene until this cross was given back to him. While aware of Albus not far behind me, I was forced to look mostly at Jesus, who increasingly struggled to keep his balance as he grew weaker before my eyes.

At times, I saw Jesus look over the crowd and even turn his head and look toward me and the prisoners just behind me. I had never seen such sorrow in anyone. His look disturbed me because I began to feel a sorrow for him that made it hard for me to look at Albus and his prisoners in the same way. I did everything I could to distract myself from my own sorrow. I even roughly bounced the cross on my shoulder, wincing with pain as I tried to break the spell of Jesus's look.

My daydreaming was interrupted by a collective gasp from the crowd. I saw Jesus once more on the stone street, lying prone this time, unmoving. I stopped just short of him. Had he simply died, and the fall was just an insignificant result?

"Ha, cheated of your crucifixion! Too bad," said the cursing prisoner sarcastically. "You've still got me, though," he added as both Albus and the younger prisoner moved quickly past me. Neither seemed to know what to do.

The angry older prisoner, though, was clearly frightened as well, his anger seeming to wear away any sensible thoughts he might have had as he drew near his own end. Anything that disrupted the plans of the Romans surely gave him pleasure. Yet his pleasure quickly passed.

"And they let Barabbas go," he blurted out. "The no-good killer," he could be heard muttering to himself. It was indeed an outrage that Barabbas roamed the streets drunk, enjoying himself at the Passover feast.

Meanwhile, Jesus still did not move. I could see that the young criminal was terrified at the sight of Jesus's bloodied body. His knees began to shake visibly. I wasn't prepared for what happened next. Albus reached out and steadied him for just a moment, and then quickly withdrew his arm.

I could not tell, looking at him lying on the wet stones, whether there was any sign of him breathing. Had he just died before us? I wanted nothing of his cross, nothing of its wood in my flesh, not one sliver to remind me of these hours spent like a criminal, among criminals, with the brutality of Rome cracking its whip repeatedly over my life.

"That's it—that's three hard falls," announced a Roman guard. "Fall again, Nazarene, and I'll run you through myself with my spear," he said, though I hardly believed he had such authority.

"No you won't!" Gustus shouted out at the guard, who quickly turned away.

Abenadar, hearing Gustus's reprimand of his soldier, quickly rode up and intervened. "Get the prisoner to his feet," he commanded Albus.

Both Albus and the younger prisoner quickly grabbed Jesus under his arms and around his chest, lifting him up.

I now was so close to Jesus that I heard Albus mutter to Jesus,

"You've got to keep going. They would just as soon kill you here." Then he turned abruptly away, ordering the other two prisoners to fall in line behind me. Abenadar nodded his approval and rode off, and I noticed he never looked my way.

Albus had surprised me. It didn't make sense. Confused by his warning to Jesus, I wondered why Albus would say anything to him at all. And he almost seemed to be befriending him.

Having put the cross down, I rushed to Jesus, trying to steady the exhausted man. Careful not to be punctured by another of the thorns in his head, I looked closely at the cruel mockery of a crown he still wore. The thorns were roughly the length of my small finger, but only a part of each one was exposed. They bore deeply into his scalp and forehead, often sliding sideways when they reached the bone and could not fight the resistance. They then slanted into his flesh. Beneath his hairline, I could see the raised skin in places where the thorn had settled, nestling into a firm grip in his bloody scalp.

I looked at several on the back of his head, where there was a little more flesh on his scalp. Ugly purple bruises gathered at the base of the thorns. Their centers were red and bruised, surrounding deep punctures, like a nail driven into very soft wood that had split under the stress of the impact. So many of them, spaced unevenly, had begun to swell Jesus's skull. Tightly drawn, the skin had changed the shape of his head in a grotesque way. It was hard to look at him now.

Jesus said nothing. He didn't even try to ease the pain by lifting the crown from his head so that the thorns would not be embedded so deeply in his scalp. Suffering deeply, Jesus's face showed his agony, but his eyes revealed something else. I saw calmness in him, a quiet determination to make this journey and be nailed to the cross, taking in all that was required. These thoughts moved through me as I carefully released him. He stopped swaying.

I returned to the cross. I was determined to take up the weight and the terror of the cross once again. I shuddered at the brutality of it all as I bent low to get underneath it. Then, with leg muscles beginning to quiver and shake under the sustained load, I lifted the cross with my shoulder so that the tip of its crossbeam rose above the heads of the people. They appeared to follow its lead as though we were all in a sort of daydream, and that state had become the hard reality of our journey.

Behind me, I could hear Albus talking to the younger prisoner, although it was hard to understand what he was saying as his words twisted their way out across his mutilated tongue. Yet as I glanced back, I saw that the younger prisoner seemed to be attending to his every word, while to all appearances, Albus was roughly pushing the prisoners forward.

I did not know what to make of this. Did Albus know the Nazarene? And what did he have to say to the young criminal? I began to feel even more uneasy with Albus walking behind me. My hatred now mingled with confusion about what I had heard and seen him do. Surely he couldn't be a follower of Jesus. I know I had heard that Jesus had followers among the Romans. Yet surely not among the soldiers. Not Albus. It couldn't be possible. I quickly put the nagging thought behind me as we passed through the city gates and began the climb up the hill to Golgotha.

XX

Passing through the city gates thrust us into another realm. Most of the members of the dwindling crowd simply stopped at the gates, evidently not wanting to go farther. I figured they had seen enough. I concentrated on the climb. Follower or not, Albus had killed Pricilla and helped abduct Alexander. Yet I was disturbed by what I had seen. I did not understand his peculiar behavior with Jesus, and when I glanced back at Albus, I could see him looking mostly at him.

Forced to follow Jesus, I had no choice in the matter, but watching Jesus struggle up the hill, I understood how his suffering could draw us all toward him. I had been forced to carry his cross, forced to follow him. Why would someone choose to follow him? I admitted to myself that his path of sorrow seemed so at odds with my desire for revenge. When I looked at him struggle up the hill, it was harder for me to focus on Albus. My full attention became riveted on Jesus as we reached Golgotha.

We suddenly came upon Golgotha. Rocky and unusually quiet, it was desolate, like an abandoned piece of land. Two crosses lay on the ground. A few priests and scribes had already gathered to see their condemned man, the one they believed had blasphemed against Yahweh and the Jewish law, crucified.

A few of the soldiers turned and rode off. Gustus called Abenadar to him. "Abenadar," I heard him shout, "I don't need you! Leave the pale one, Albus, here to see this through. Report back to Pilate. Tell him it's almost over."

Abenadar nodded his head. I saw him say a few words to Albus, pull hard on his horse's reins, and ride off. I told myself that at least I now knew he was here in Jerusalem. There would be another time to deal with him. I was glad to be rid of him, for now I could focus on Albus and not worry about Abenadar interfering.

I would have my chance at Albus. I noticed, however, that he seemed to hang back from the other soldiers, and again I saw him looking at Jesus. I was surprised at how boyish and open his face appeared. He seemed younger than I remembered. He stood close to the two other prisoners, watching Jesus and struggling to speak clearly to the youngest criminal. At times, they both looked at Jesus as though they had nowhere else to look and nothing more to say.

Jesus was breathing heavily. A Pharisee mocked him and said to no one in particular, "He saved others. Why can't he save himself?"

Another from the crowd chimed in, "The chosen one? Chosen to die."

Some began to laugh among themselves. "Go on," one of them goaded, "climb the cross. Proclaim your kingship now!"

Jesus turned and gestured for me to bring the cross to where the two other crosses were lying on the ground. I kept silent as Jesus nodded toward the spot where the cross would be lowered in the ground. It was a shallow hole used many times. I hesitated. Strangely, I thought that if I held on to the cross, they wouldn't crucify him. A soldier gave me a push, and I stumbled forward and put the cross down slowly. I then backed away. This cross no longer belonged to me, or so it seemed. I didn't have to carry it any farther.

Jesus watched me as I backed away, and our eyes met. I saw once again a bottomless sorrow in his eyes. It enveloped me in the moment, causing me to sink unexpectedly to my knees. What more could I do for him? The cross was out of my hands.

The crowd circled around us now. I heard the younger condemned man ask Albus, "Do you know which cross I will be on?"

"No, son, I do not," answered Albus, struggling to articulate each word. Albus stood so close to me now that I thought I could reach around, grab him under the chin, draw my knife, and slit his throat in an instant. Yet I hesitated. I couldn't do it in front of this terrified young criminal. Albus's obvious care for the younger criminal felt strange to me. The moment passed quickly.

"I wonder if I could choose my cross?" the young man asked, clearly frightened and shivering, certainly less from the cold wind beginning to blow harder than from what he knew was about to happen to him.

"I'll ask the commander," Albus replied. He quickly turned and walked to Gustus. I could hear Albus's stuttering request.

"The request is granted," answered Gustus in an exaggerated official way, while I heard him mutter under his breath, "Who cares, anyway? Death is death."

Another guard found Albus's request for the criminal amusing. "Yes, to the right of the son of God, if you wish, young man. It will be easier there for you," he said, laughing.

Jesus had been standing there listening to this exchange. He looked over to the young man. The prisoner's legs were shaking. His face was suddenly pale, and occasionally a shiver went through his body as he looked at the cross on the ground, the one he had asked to die on. He seemed to be asking us all if we had to do this, while knowing the answer full well.

Jesus turned toward the trembling young man. "You will soon be with me in a far better realm," he said.

Surprisingly, Jesus nodded at Albus, who stood next to the young man. Albus backed away, as if not wanting to recognize him in return in front of the other soldiers. The thought again raced through my mind that he had become one of Jesus's followers. How could that be? Kill my wife. Take my son. And then this. A secret follower of this Jesus of Nazareth? Did Albus think "the past" could just be washed away by this Nazarene who himself was about to die? Maybe he wasn't a follower. Maybe I was mistaken. How could I, though, if I didn't know for sure, kill a follower of this suffering man? It didn't make sense, and I felt the ground of my grief and anger pulled from beneath me. Bewildered, I watched the scene unfold.

The young criminal had cast his eyes to the ground when he heard Jesus's words. His breathing grew more even, less strained and shallow. His heart seemed calmed by Jesus's words. No longer shaking, he kept focused on Jesus instead of looking down at his own cross. Another realm? What did Jesus mean? How could that comfort this young man when nails would be driven through his flesh in a few moments?

The air now smelled of death, of blood, of suffering and unspeakable pain. I had brought my own anger and grief to this hill, a hill of death, and Jesus was in the midst of it all. He was standing before us with a look of sorrow and compassion, as if embracing my anger and grief. The two criminals, Albus, and the few followers who had come to Golgotha clustered in a circle.

It was as though Jesus was saying that death would go no further than him, if you followed him. Whatever his power, it seemed to be defying the terror in us all at the moment, defying our fear with an all-embracing love. I couldn't move. I did not understand the power that emanated from this man who was about to die on a cross a few feet from me, the one I had carried to this hill.

Watching Jesus stand next to his cross along with the two criminals about to be executed, I began to feel overwhelmed. It was too much to absorb. I couldn't. Yet it seemed that was just what Jesus was doing: absorbing the death we had all brought to this place, where the skulls of countless criminals had been crushed to death.

I realized then that this Jesus of Nazareth now stood between Albus and me. I felt that my plans were being thwarted, as if I could not keep going back into my anger in the presence of the compassion I saw in Jesus of Nazareth. The grip of my angry past began to loosen its stranglehold on my life. Jesus had drawn me forward, into the present, into what was about to happen.

XXI

Abruptly stripped of his garments by two soldiers, but with Albus not helping them, Jesus fought to keep his balance with only a cloth around his loins. He did not resist. He looked helpless and even more vulnerable than he had a few moments before, as though he had lost a small bit of protection from what was about to happen to him.

I saw a look of pity cross Albus's face. I quickly looked away. Had he no pity for Pricilla? Now he was reluctantly following orders, and yet with Pricilla he couldn't resist Abenadar's orders. Anger flared through my body yet passed quickly. Jesus stood only a few steps away, only moments from being nailed to the cross. I too had followed orders.

Jesus's body, mutilated by repeated beatings, appeared so thin and pale, his skin not unlike Albus's pale demeanor. His ribs stuck out against his skin, giving him a gaunt appearance. A great dread came over me. I was keenly aware that Jesus was about to leave us for good.

A vague sense of guilt engulfed me. How could I have desired to kill another man, Albus, when this innocent man was about to be crucified on the very cross I'd carried for him? I understood the anger and grief I'd felt right after Pricilla's death, and the pain of my son being suddenly taken away, but kill another person? How could I plan to do that, even Abenadar or Albus? What would Pricilla say? What good would that do? And before Jesus, this seemed to be so terribly wrong, as did even the lesser crimes of my heart through the years. Was there no innocence left in me?

Albus issued an order to the soldiers. "Get on with it," he said. "The time has come. You'll not torture the prisoners by stalling." Albus stuttered through his words, and one soldier mocked him by pretending that he couldn't understand. It was then that I saw Albus's anger suddenly appear. The soldiers moved the other crosses into place.

Gustus rode up. "Albus, you'd make a good leader, if only you could talk. You're in charge here now. You know what to do. I'm reporting back to Pilate. Report to me when it's over, or send someone to tell me. Understand?"

Albus nodded. Gustus pulled hard on the reins of his horse, which fought him for a moment, and then he quickly turned and rode off, leaning back in his saddle as he descended the hill toward Jerusalem.

My mind raced to make sense of it all but could not. I hadn't chosen to carry this cross. It was hardly my intention. Quite the contrary. It had fallen across my path, blocking my murderous plans. I had only consented to the Roman order. What choice did I have? Then I had embraced my task, especially as I saw the horrible treatment of this Jesus of Nazareth. I wasn't guilty ... or was there some sense in which I still felt so guilty before his innocence? I had plenty of regrets, enough to feel guilty about.

I stood there amidst all the commotion of getting three men crucified in the shortest time possible, feeling numb toward what was around me. I was paralyzed, uncertain, bewildered by it all. I could still kill Albus. I told myself I had plenty of time. I now had access to him, and I knew I would in the moments that followed. Yet looking at Jesus, stripped almost naked and about to be crucified, I had no desire in me to carry out my plans right then. I'd still have time later. Now Rome was done with me. I was expendable, like a pack animal that had carried its burden and could now be dismissed. But I stayed, unable to turn away.

The small crowd parted. A few women pushed through and moved near Jesus. Albus did not object. I immediately recognized Jesus's mother, Mary, who'd folded his clothes in her arms, only to have them suddenly yanked from her by one of the soldiers now under the command of Albus.

"Let's cast lots for these," he announced. "Let the prisoner wait awhile." Two other guards immediately sat down, and they played their game, mocking Jesus by pretending his clothing was worth so much.

The game didn't last long. Albus told them to stop. "Get on with the punishment," he ordered.

"Yes, Commander," one of the soldiers responded, imitating Albus's mangled speech. So quickly you've been promoted. You seem to like the prisoners more than us." He laughed loudly while Albus glared at him.

Jesus stood with his head bowed. His hair fell down over his face as though hiding him from the mockery of the soldiers. It was apparent now that with Abenadar gone, and the commander of the procession, Gustus, having fulfilled his duties and having left as well, Albus was left in charge with a few guards who resented Albus's new stature and position.

Was I to simply watch Albus while he ordered the killing of this innocent man? The crucifixions were routine matters. He had his orders, and yet it seemed as if he wanted nothing to do with what was happening. The others appeared to sense that. Yet he had to carry out the orders of Gustus. Not a pleasant task but not one of the worst assignments. Jesus was providing the few other remaining soldiers with an amusing diversion, at least for a while. Some small reward for the long journey to Golgotha. Stripped of all dignity, Jesus shivered in the cold while the soldiers stalled in spite of Albus's orders and playfully gambled for his clothing.

Mary appeared from the small crowd and went to Jesus. Albus didn't interfere. She reached up to her son's face, took her shawl, and much like Veronica, tenderly wiped the sweat and blood from his face. I couldn't hear what they were saying. Mary, however, seemed calmed by his words. Jesus's shivering increased in the damp air, which had turned colder.

Looking at Jesus with his mother and then scanning those around me, I knew that somehow we had all become a part of this procession, this long caravan of people: Pilate, the crowd, onlookers, Veronica, Mary, the thief, the young man who'd helped me with the cross … I wondered if James was somewhere around, watching us all. And all the onlookers: the poor, the beggars, the blind, the children, the possessed … We were all here. Jesus, it seemed, with a power in his vulnerability, through his simple love and acceptance, included us all within this march. Was this to be the end of it all?

For me? For my sons as well? A story of brutality, tragedy, and terrible human anguish? Here I stood, not far from the man who had killed my own wife, and not far away in my heart the desire to kill him as well. How was it that we had all been pulled into this moment at Golgotha?

I could not comprehend how these soldiers I had begun to hate, including Albus, would someday be stripped of their weapons and armor and would lie helpless and dying in some disgraceful or painful way, perhaps in a battle for the Roman Empire. Seeing Jesus standing naked before his cross, I suddenly felt agony arising in me for Pricilla and my sons and my own life.

From deep within me, I wanted to cry out to someone, somewhere, to the God of my ancestors. Why must we, why must Jesus, die such a terrible death? Everything seemed taken from him. What kind of God would order any of us to bear such suffering and death? Did I really need to be shown my own vulnerable humanity through this man's approaching torment on the cross? What for? It hardly made sense.

I looked at the two other prisoners about to be executed. They stood by themselves. The angry criminal spat toward the crowd and jeered at those who looked at him, vainly trying to build some barrier of hate against his own fate. "You can't wait to hear us scream from the cross, can you?" he shouted. Even the crowd recognized the fear in his taunting, and from time to time, Jesus looked sadly in his direction.

A few others in the crowd swore back at him as if responding to a wild caged animal safe to tease. A few young men picked up loose stones lying around and hurled them at him. Albus quickly intervened. The mist thickened, and the gloom of this triple execution settled deeper into the darkening air. Now sounds of thunder punctuated the air; lightning flashed across the sky. I felt the fear of death deep in my bones. It was all around me. I felt once more the deep loss of Pricilla, the woman who was supposed to grow old with me.

I felt the impending death of Jesus the most acutely. In this short time, since I was compelled to carry his cross, he had become such a mysterious presence. His cross would be driven into this barren, seemingly forsaken land. Hard-packed dirt, an unforgiving earth, it had absorbed so much blood through the years, soaked in the misery of so many unknown, forgotten, and so-called criminals. I walked on death, on the blood-soaked earth, and felt its palpable presence in the air I breathed.

The only response I could think to make, short of fleeing down the side of this hill of skulls, was to walk over to the younger prisoner who stood near Albus. I put my arm around his shoulder. I wanted to console him as I would my own sons. "I will not leave," I said to him, "until all is over." Strangely, I began to feel assured that Jesus was not going to leave us either. He would not leave us with our fears, our anger, or our confusion. Somehow, he had included it all in our march to Golgotha.

The young man put his head closer to me and asked, "Why me? Why is this happening to me?" He looked around to see if anyone else could hear him, and then he whispered to me as though his life depended on it. "Do you think he's *The One*? I need to know," he pleaded.

His question, coming so innocently and directly at me, made me hesitate before answering. I knew it would help him if I could be certain. But how could I be? I could say that I really didn't know. Earlier I would have said no without hesitation. I couldn't say it now. I looked at this young man about to die. What should I do? Should I comfort him with a lie, or what could be a lie, or tell him the truth? I could not decide, but even as I continued to think of how to answer, I suddenly heard myself saying, as if a voice from another part of me wanted to speak, "He may be The One. It's possible. I don't know for sure. But you will know."

To my surprise, this answer appeared to comfort his anguish and wonder—and then mine as well. I realized there was a time for each of us to know what we needed to know. The time was different for each of us. Perhaps he understood this in a way that I did not yet comprehend. Perhaps someday, in another time and place, I would find this truth applied to my life.   •

Some in the crowd began to repeat their earlier chant directed at Jesus: "Crucify him! Crucify him!" But their shallow chanting carried little conviction now. It sounded hollow before the reality of what was happening. Their desires were being fulfilled, and the wind seemed to scatter their chants across the hill, away toward Jerusalem and beyond.

Jesus had moved away from his mother, but she stood looking

longingly at him. As soon as he looked away from her, the soldiers moved in and grabbed him from behind. Albus led Mary away to be comforted by two women standing by. "Let him go, Mary," one of them said gently. "It is now time. You've got to let him go."

The soldiers grabbed Jesus rather roughly and said, "Let's get on with it. Get the spikes and grab this so-called Messiah. Put him closer to his heaven."

"Here," said one of them, handing a roughly inscribed piece of wood to his subordinate. "Orders from Pilate. This is to be nailed at the top of the cross, above the Nazarene's head. Do it now, before we put him on the cross." It read JESUS OF NAZARETH, KING OF THE JEWS. It was his epitaph. Was it true or false? I could not say for sure. I did know I would not leave now for anything. I would stay and, if nothing else, try to comfort his mother and her companions.

A young soldier took the wooden plaque, and gazing at it with indifference, turned it over in his hands as he walked over to the cross. He took two small spikes from a pouch hanging from his uniform. With his helmet bobbing to the rhythm of the hammer blows, he drove in two nails on either side of the plaque, after placing it high so that Jesus's head wouldn't conceal it. I shuddered after hearing the first sound of nails piercing into the wood, and I turned away as I imagined what was ahead. "There, now everyone will know who you are!" the soldier said. He stepped back to admire his work.

The crowd grew silent. Jesus was pushed toward his cross, though he offered no resistance. I'd heard others say that this was when prisoners, even the bravest ones, began to struggle the most. Some had been known to try to run in the hopes of being quickly killed. Some prisoners simply began to weep, begging for a mercy they would not receive. The guards were especially alert, someone had told me, in case a small band of Jesus's friends suddenly bolted from the crowd to free him. Word was that Jesus had many disciples. Could Albus possibly be one of them? I still could not think that possible, and yet I was no longer sure.

I heard Albus tell the soldiers, "No need to push him. Can't you see? He goes willingly. Hands off the prisoner."

Jesus turned and looked at Albus. In that moment, I knew. Albus must be a follower.

XXI

Jesus stumbled, fell, and then crawled the short remaining distance to the cross. He hesitated for a moment before straddling it with his legs and arms. Embracing the cross for a moment, he let go, turned himself over, and lay flat on his back on the splintered wood. Grimacing from the wounds in his deeply lacerated back, he held still for a moment.

He then stretched his arms out to each side of the crossbeam. In that moment, I sensed his acceptance of all of the agony inflicted upon his innocent life. My arms crossed over my chest. I began to wonder about myself, including the anger I felt at Albus, the Roman soldier who stood so close. The grief I felt for Pricilla and my missing son seemed to be pinned to this cross as well, and yet how could I accept the horror of that night in Cyrene? I found it hard to look at Jesus with his arms so willingly stretched out upon the cross as he now accepted the inevitable.

As I was only a short distance from Jesus, I saw the broken and torn skin on his chest and legs. The light rain began to cover his body and make his skin shine as if coated lightly with oil. He shivered in the cold and the dampness. His face remained calm as he looked skyward from time to time. He waited.

His flesh would soon be nailed to the wood. I had dreaded this moment back in the streets of Jerusalem. Now the moment had arrived. No wonder I had thought to put the cross down and rush headlong back to the city without another word. But I couldn't leave now. Nausea suddenly spread through me. I began to perspire profusely. The sweat dripped off my forehead.

"First time I've seen a prisoner place himself on the cross," mused one of the soldiers. "It's almost as if he wanted to be crucified. How could any human being wish that on himself? Makes our task easier." He fidgeted in his leather sack for the spikes he would use on Jesus.

Still there was jeering. "Save yourself if you are such a king," some taunted. "You say you can save others, but you can't save yourself."

His mother was sobbing and being held by two other women. She had turned her head away and buried it in the shoulder of the older of the two. Other women stood near Mary, weeping as well. Some of the crowd looked the other way. A hush fell over everyone. I felt a deep pain settle in my heart, and in that moment, some depth of anger and grief drained out of me. A sudden gust of wind arose, sweeping around us. It went through me as well, drying the sweat on my brow but sending through me a chill I couldn't escape.

The soldiers methodically took out the spikes and laid them alongside the cross. Albus seemed intent on making his death occur as quickly as possible. It startled me to think that this was his way of helping the Nazarene while pretending to be one more soldier doing an unpleasant task. "Work fast," he said. "Let's get this over." The others nodded their assent.

As he spoke, a guard quickly took Jesus's left arm and stretched it along the rain-soaked blackened wood. Jesus allowed it to happen, as though simply giving his arm over to the guard. He looked in the direction of the guard and then to the palm of his hand. The rancid smell of blood from others who had died on this cross suddenly sickened me further. Two other guards grabbed Jesus's feet and aligned his thin white legs, which were wounded by the markings of whips and bruised purple from the kicks of several soldiers.

"The larger spikes first," Albus ordered. "For his feet."

For some reason, the guards and Albus appeared hesitant, looking back and forth between Jesus and the spikes in their hands.

Jesus looked intently at Albus, "Go ahead," he said in a gentle yet commanding voice, which seemed to relieve Albus and the guards as well.

Then came the first blow. At the sound of the hammer hitting the nail and driving through the flesh of Jesus into the wooden cross, I gasped for air. Albus stepped back, wincing himself as he watched the soldiers at work, unable to look at Jesus. And then a terrible howl pierced the air as Mary cried out, "No! No! Don't do this to him! Don't you know what you're doing?" And then her cry broke into sobbing. The two women pulled her closer and held her tightly. More sounds of hammer on nails caused me to cringe with each blow. Jesus's body convulsed with every strike.

The guards worked efficiently. I, like many others, had to turn my head and face into the wind, hoping that its noise would block the sound of the relentless hammering. I could not watch the brutality of this crucifixion, especially not this one. But while I could avert my eyes from the horrid sight, I could not block my ears to the sounds of the hammers driven first through flesh until the nails rested in the wood with a dull thud, where the sound thickened and spread itself deep, fastening him securely. Mercifully, the thunder rumbled in our direction. At times, the thunder absorbed the hammer blows as if the heavens themselves had conspired to absorb this cruelty enacted on Earth. At no time in all this did I hear Jesus cry out. With each blow of the hammer, however, I heard a short, low moan and two or three times a deep sighing sound as he deeply exhaled.

I turned to watch the body of Jesus quivering under the spikes that pinned him to the cross. I thought of Pricilla. Did she thrash about when she could not bear the pain of the soldiers tearing their lust into her body? Just like this? A wave of sympathy overwhelmed me. Looking at Albus, I saw his head bowed. His shoulders slumped forward. For the first time, I wondered how such a young man had been swept up into killing my wife. He looked suddenly younger and even more boyish. Much to my surprise, I saw him quickly wipe tears from his face with the back of his hand while looking about to see if anyone had noticed.

My moment of sympathy for him passed quickly, yet it had taken hold in me. I knew neither Jesus nor Pricilla deserved their agonizing deaths. I felt suddenly bewildered by the sight of Jesus's wounded body. Looking at him, I no longer found comfort in my anger. The ground seemed to shift beneath me. What sense did this suffering make? How could Jesus accept what had happened to him? Was there no justice on Earth? Life was hard enough … and then this. It was unfair.

What God would allow this suffering to happen to anyone? Did

God feel the pain of Pricilla and these other criminals as well? Was God so powerless? What power did God have, anyway? If this Jesus was The One, was this the power he had come to show us? My mind and heart were suddenly assaulted with questions I could not answer. Yet it haunted me that there was something about God's power that I didn't understand. What was it? Could he be telling us something about the power to be affected? The power to feel deeply the pain of our vulnerable lives? In surrendering the power over the world and receiving our pain, was Jesus transforming the unfair cruelty being driven into his body into a new way of life we couldn't comprehend? I didn't know. I couldn't think more at the moment.

The other two prisoners now stood horrified before their crosses as they watched Jesus. The younger shook throughout his body. The older criminal suddenly caved into the moment and fell to his knees. Albus quickly ordered them to be crucified. They, unlike Jesus, were both dragged to their crosses and held down while the sounds of hammers blended with their cries of excruciating pain.

As the dull thud of the hammers nailing Jesus and the two thieves to the crosses sounded above the thunder that rose in the nearby hills, another deafening silence descended on the crowd. I could still hear Jesus's mother sobbing with the two women, and some very young children were grasping their mothers' robes.

I hid my face in my hands, and the tears streamed over them. Did Jesus somehow grasp my own suffering and my own agony? In some strange way, what was happening to him was happening to me, for I felt my love for and loss of my family. The only power he had to give me, or that I ever needed, was the power of his steadfast love in spite of all this hatred. I began to feel some relief that I had not experienced since Pricilla's death.

The guards finished hammering. The ropes and pulleys were now in place; the men, breathing heavily, shouted orders to one another. They began to lift Jesus's cross toward the thundering clouds. Bearing its own weight and the weight of Jesus, it slid into the hollow of the hole and stopped abruptly with a loud thud, muffled partly by the earth into which it sank. Hanging on the cross, Jesus's body came to a jolting halt. Writhing in my own pain, I could barely look at Jesus's agonizing suffering.

XXIII

Still conscious, but now closer to death than life, Jesus hung there. Within a few moments, my world swirled around me as I watched this innocent man suffer his cruel execution. Braced on a small block of wood, cut on an angle, it supported his feet and body. A large spike held each foot firmly to the wood block. Blood oozed from around the spikes. Looking up, I saw the same was true of his wrists. Jesus's head fell forward. He gasped for breath. Fully soaked by the rain and his sweat, his hair partially hid his face. Tears flowed from his eyes. Eyes half opened, he strained to look around from time to time. Involuntary spasms wracked his body. He occasionally threw his head from side to side. Helplessness mixed with my own anger. The horror of his crucifixion made me want to turn and run from the place.

For a moment, I wished Albus would simply run him through with his spear, but he too stood transfixed by Jesus, who seemed to look upon me as though he knew my sorrow for him. My own pain seemed to mingle with his. As much as I told myself that my suffering was not his, I could not escape the feeling that there was something about his dying that involved not only me. What could I do? I hated my helplessness. I felt a sudden compassion for this suffering man with the innocence in his face battling the pain in his body. I was not alone in being drawn into his suffering.

Jesus's mother and her friends had now gathered with me at the foot of the cross. I looked up at him, and he looked down from a place I saw in his eyes—a place that was much farther away than the short distance that separated us. I watched him breathe in and out in rapid succession. I knew that he had already slowly begun to suffocate. Gasping for air, he couldn't get enough, and it was as though he were drowning on the cross.

I had never seen such agony. How could my sons have been able to tolerate witnessing what had been done to their mother? Anger flared through me again, yet it quickly passed before the agony of Jesus. I noticed how his body was splayed out as if in a gesture of openness. What did he have to receive from us now? What could I do? Excruciating dismay and attraction welled up in me simultaneously. I felt ashamed at the mixed feelings that swirled through me like a frigid wind. They were hard to sort out.

I cared nothing for the soldiers now. I moved closer to Albus. I had no fear he would recognize me, especially now, as he seemed totally intent on carrying out his orders, even though he appeared strangely reluctant to do so. I didn't care. My own fear had been abolished. I felt reckless, and I once again touched the handle of my knife, taking comfort that it was still there. I was thinking again that the stupid soldiers had never once thought to search me.

The small band, including Jesus's mother, who could no longer stand without support from her friends, had gathered closely together. I heard Mary cry out, "Why, why are they doing this to him? They're killing my son. Killing my son!" Then her agonizing cry convulsed into deeper sobbing.

Nailed to their crosses and writhing to escape the pain, the other two prisoners tossed about in agony and shrieks of pain. Jesus looked to them on his right and left, which seemed to soothe their struggling. They still fought back, the one criminal cursing his pain, while they both yielded their bodies to the relentless agony of their individual crosses.

The metallic smell of blood was heavy in the air. Something both unnatural and human caused my nostrils to flare. The blood appeared to be draining faster from Jesus. The sooner that happened, the sooner he would die, escaping his misery.

There was no question. I had to stay until Jesus died. I, who lived always in the shadow of a mild fear without any real object of fear, had found myself on a path hardly of my own choosing. Pricilla's death had buried for good my timidity about life. I had the resolve to kill

Albus, yet I was now haunted by the thought that he himself might be a follower of Jesus. How did that fit into what was happening now?

Watching Jesus die, a surge of hope surprisingly swept through me. I began to feel an equally powerful resolve to get out of the situation alive, no matter how it turned out with Albus. My anger over the loss of Pricilla had turned into a resolve to live. I still had to find my son Alexander. And there was Rufus and his family … and my grandchildren. Yes, I was at this cross for Pricilla. I had fully intended to take a life for her life. Jesus crossed my path, threw his life in front of me, and I had to carry his bloody cross. For me. For Pricilla. Blood would still be spilled. I would do everything I could to make sure it was not mine, not yet.

I looked at Albus, who stood surveying the scene before him. He himself seemed to be gasping for air, breathing hard, as though in some rhythmic sympathy with Jesus. I became conscious of my own steady breathing. Were we not all, together, breathing the air Jesus was breathing? I realized how close I was to the moment when I too would exhale my final breath. Perhaps not today. Perhaps not tomorrow. Some day, not far away, I too would breathe my last.

The defiant older criminal suddenly taunted Jesus, "King of the Jews, where's your power now?"

A few of the crowd began to chant, "Come down from the cross, come down from the cross." Their cries were met by Jesus's silence. He seemed to look through the crowd to his mother, who could not look at him, for she had buried her head in her hands and knelt on the ground, surrounded by the other women.

A burly older guard suddenly turned to Albus and, putting his face close to his, started giving Albus orders. "Let's go, Albus. This show's over. Unless you've got something for him, we've done enough."

Albus ordered him to stay. He stood staring at Albus, hand on his sword, and I thought a fight would ensue. With a smirk, the muscular guard slowly turned and joined the other guards at the crosses.

The younger condemned man suddenly looked over at Jesus and pleaded with him as he struggled now for his own breath. "Jesus, remember me when you come into your kingdom," he pleaded. It was clear that no one expected this from the young criminal. Jesus had said nothing up to that point, only listening to us while often focused on his mother. His breathing now became more shallow and forced.

He turned his head slightly to his right in a struggle to see the young man's face. Jesus gasped for air as he struggled to speak. His breath was even more constricted as the weight of his body pulled him down. "I promise you," he said to the young man, "that you will be with me in paradise." Shivering, the young man continued to gaze at Jesus. I stood in silence, astonished at the words exchanged between the two condemned men, in spite of the agonizing effort it took for them to speak.

Now the wind increased, as though snatching these words and carrying them across the land, down toward the city, and away into the vast desert. Could the desert yield a paradise? In the midst of all this horror, would life get better for me, for those of us clustered around these dying men? Perhaps my mind couldn't take this anymore. I don't know. I envisioned springs in the desert. For a moment, I saw a desert beginning to bloom. I saw people returning to Jerusalem, singing and rejoicing as they entered the holy city as though made new, and now living in a world of love and justice. I saw Pricilla, and Rufus, and Alexander, my sisters-in-law, my grandchildren. I saw the blind, the poor, the beggars, the lepers. I saw soldiers and a young child leading the way.

Surprised by this sudden vision, I had the crazy thought that even now in his presence, another world was already in the making. I was entering into it through imaginings like this, which were as close to me as my breath, the spirit of God blowing through me like the wind and forming me out of desert dust, breathing new life into my own grief-shattered life. This vision seemed for a moment to blur the painful dying of someone who had drawn so much hatred toward him, and yet who had not cursed even one of us, not one.

XXIV

Jesus had been quiet. Still gasping for breath, he looked from side to side at the prisoners hanging next to him, and then at times he seemed to be gazing at us with a far-off look. A few of us moved closer to him, including Mary and the other women who continued to hold her. Albus now stood only a few feet away, watching the dying Jesus. Not far behind us, a few soldiers sat in a circle, passing the common drink of the soldiers, sour wine mixed with gall. It was having its effect, rendering them close to senseless as they occasionally mocked the prisoners while speaking louder to each other, pushing their faces close to the next man's.

"Albus," the burly soldier, who had just threatened him called out. "Come drink with us. Bring your wine. Let the prisoners alone."

Then he turned to the other soldiers, and I heard him say, "I think he's a follower. Look at him staring at Jesus." The other soldiers turned to look. They drank more wine. I noticed them murmuring something among themselves that I couldn't make out.

"Oh, Albus," the leader of the soldiers called out, "are you going to drink with us or help your friend Jesus die?" Albus turned and looked at him and the group of soldiers but didn't reply. I looked away, and back toward Jesus, but I continued to hear the soldiers as they drank more and continued to jeer at Jesus and now at Albus as well. Albus ignored them.

Mary and the other women also ignored the remaining soldiers and kept their attention on Jesus. "He's speaking," said one of the women. Along with them, I looked up to Jesus, but now the wind had grown so strong we couldn't hear his words. He didn't seem to be speaking to us. I strained to listen, but I could only hear him repeating the word "father." Then I thought I heard him say "forgive." I was surprised to see Albus suddenly move closer to the cross, as though he had heard something none of us could discern.

Then Jesus was silent. Motionless, the two prisoners hung heavily on their crosses, and suddenly Jesus cried out in agonizing pain, "My God, why have you forsaken me?"

Mary broke into tears at his agonizing words seemingly tossed into the empty sky above.

Albus quickly emptied his flask of sour wine and gall on a sponge, dousing it with enough sour wine to numb Jesus's acute agony. Albus thrust his spear through the sponge and quickly hoisted it to the mouth of Jesus. I wanted Jesus to suck it all in and relieve his terrible agony, numbing his mind and body all at once.

With a steady hand, Albus held the spear near his lips. Jesus looked down at him. He nodded his head toward him, plainly recognizing what he was doing. Amazingly, he then simply took a sip of the sour wine mixed with gall, thereby acknowledging the attempted gift of relief from Albus. His head recoiled a bit from the bitterness of the gall. At the same time, he shook his head. He would not drink enough wine to dull his senses. Jesus would not relieve himself of his suffering. Albus seemed to understand instantly.

No sooner had Albus lowered his spear than three of the soldiers suddenly seized him from behind. Their older leader clasped his hand over Albus's mouth and lifted him off the ground, while the two others quickly bound his arms and legs. They dragged him forcefully back through the crowd, which parted in fear, allowing the soldiers to pass.

It all happened so quickly. I turned and began to follow them at a distance as they dragged Albus away from the crowd and a short way down the hill. What were they up to? Sure, they were annoyed with him. Was it any of my business? The crowd looked confused by the soldiers' actions, but it was clear the people wanted no part of it, for they turned back to the crucifixions.

"You're his follower!" I heard their leader shout, followed by curses from the other soldiers. "This is what happens to those who betray Rome."

I stood paralyzed, not knowing what to do as I saw a sword raised.

Before I could do anything, I heard a muffled cry from down the hill; it was quickly swept away by the wind. Moments later, the three soldiers made their way back up the hill. I saw their leader wiping blood off his sword. I got out of their way. They took no note of me as they passed more wine among themselves on their way back to the crosses. Drinking may have made their violence swifter and easier to commit.

I rushed down the hill to Albus, who was curled up next to a huge boulder. He was lying on his back in a pool of blood; his left leg was askew, as though it had been broken. Tears flowed down his cheeks, and for some strange reason, he resembled my son Alexander at that moment. I reached into my robe, grasped my knife, and hurled it down the hill while rushing to his side. I knelt next to him and cradled his head in my arms.

He looked me in the eyes and struggled to speak as I saw clearly where the edge of his tongue had been bitten off. He could barely keep his eyes open as he looked at me. "I am his follower. I am," he said, barely able to whisper the words. "He forgave me," he went on. "I know he forgave me."

Then Albus looked me directly in the eyes and, with a painful, quizzical look, and seemingly summoning all his remaining strength, asked, "Do I know you?"

I paused for a moment. "No," I said. "You do not know me. But I have seen your kindness to Jesus."

A barely discernable smile crossed his face, and then Albus's body went limp, and he softly exhaled his last breath. I gently lowered him to the earth. I walked slowly back up the hill and found my way back to the cross, where I stood looking at Jesus. I was in shock. I looked but could hardly see him, for in the face of Jesus, I saw also the dying face of Albus.

My scrambled thoughts suddenly interrupted, Jesus sighed, and his words found the lull between gusts of wind. I hear him cry out, "Father, into your hands I commit my spirit." We watched as Jesus breathed his last remaining breaths and then simply said, "It is finished." His head fell to one side, and his whole body went limp on the cross.

Silence fell on the crowd, and even the drunken soldiers said nothing. For an instant, I saw my wife hanging there on the cross instead of him. Pricilla seemed to look down at me in her loving way, as though she understood it all. I thought a dream had overtaken me. I realized that the sudden shock of Albus's death, and now the death of Jesus, had thrown me into some dreamlike state. Quite suddenly, I realized that it was finished. Finished for Jesus, for Albus. It was over for me.

I would never hold that knife again. Pricilla was gone. I had to find Alexander. Return to my family. The rest was finished.

I looked at Jesus hanging from the cross. No movement. No heavy breathing. Stillness. His flesh slowly sagged toward us and bowed slightly from the cross's vertical beam. There was no tension in his arms as they collapsed into the shape of an archer's bow. His back arched away from the wood and pulled on the spikes in his hands. His feet began to tear away from the spikes, which were no longer able to hold them in place. Death's gravity pulled his body down toward us as though he was ready to fall into our arms.

Before I had time to wonder how we might remove the body of Jesus from the cross, the heavy clouds above us suddenly opened and gushed their water down on the living and the dead, including the two criminals on each side of Jesus, who had all but died their own painful deaths.

The three soldiers who had just killed Albus now stepped forward. Their leader seemed barely able to stand. They were cursing to themselves and to one another. "This day will never be over," one of them complained, slipping in the mud. "So let's get this done quickly."

Instead of a sword, one of the soldiers carried a wooden club with him. They approached as a group, and the one with the club, with a swiftness that astonished me, suddenly swung it to his side and brought it crashing against the legs of the thief on Jesus's left, venting his anger on the moaning prisoner.

He then turned to the prisoner on the right side of Jesus and bragged to his companions, "Let's see if I can break both legs with one blow."

Passing Jesus, he moved to the younger man, who was now shivering uncontrollably. The backs of his legs slapped against the wet wood.

"You're a young one … with strong bones. A good test. So stand back." With those words, he forced us away from the base of the young man's cross so we would not interrupt the wide arc of his swing. He swung his club in a complete circle before bringing it to the level of the man's shins, which we heard crack and shatter under the force of the blow. The young man was too exhausted to cry out. He simply collapsed on his cross with a deep moan.

The same soldier went to Jesus and called out to him, "King of the Jews, are you sleeping or just resting?" Getting no response, he prodded Jesus's feet with his club. "You seem dead to me. But I have my orders."

He walked over to his companion who had Albus's lance, the sponge still stuck to its end. He took it from him and carefully removed the sponge. He stepped immediately in front of Jesus, lifted the lance, and ran it into his left side. Blood mixed with a clear liquid flowed immediately from it. He quickly stepped back as it splattered his legs. The blood stained his boots as he again cursed Jesus.

"He's dead now," he said to himself, but loud enough for us to overhear him. "That finishes the three of them," he proudly announced to his companions.

Watching the lifeless body of Jesus and remembering Pricilla, I could not escape the thought of my own death. How would I face that? Would it be horrifying like this? Would it come with an inevitable force that I could not resist, like Pricilla's death? Of course, I did not know. What I did know is that my death was inevitable. None of us in that crowd or around that cross would escape our final end, yet I had the sense that his death was somehow encompassing our inevitable deaths in some way I could not understand.

I raised my left hand to my right shoulder because the cold rain had reminded me of the ache I had there from carrying the cross for so long. It felt as if it had been with me my entire life. I could not let the death of this man defeat me now. I still had something to carry for him and for myself. But something went out of me at that moment. I felt like dying—giving up and giving in. And yet there was some impulse to fight back the despair, to beat back the feelings of wanting to die. Why live in a world intent on so much cruelty? Was there no way out of this violence?

As I looked up, Jesus's lifeless body sagged even farther away from the cross, and it seemed it might tear away at any moment and fall to the ground.

Startled back to the present by a gentle hand on my shoulder, where I had once carried the cross, I turned to look into the face of the mother of Jesus. Mary stood there looking directly into my eyes, her own eyes filled with tears, red from crying. "Come, please help me with my son's body," she said, and putting her arm through mine, she gently led me closer to the foot of the cross.

XXV

The rain began to subside, and the storm rumbled past Jerusalem and into the far hills on the other side of the city. Mary and her companions began to open the shroud they had kept hidden, partly to keep it dry and also so the Roman soldiers would not take it, along with Jesus's clothing.

A lone sentry—a youthful, barely bearded, and slightly built man—who had stood apart from the drunken soldiers, and who now stayed under orders from the others who had left, brought a ladder. He leaned it against Jesus's cross. One of the men near Mary gave the guard a piece of paper. He read it and nodded his approval to the older man, who was finely dressed in a blue and gold robe. Apparently, he had been granted permission to receive the body of Jesus.

I put my weight against the ladder to steady it. The two other men stepped forward to help. They also helped hold the legs in place while the remaining guard carefully climbed the ladder.

He removed the larger spikes first from one wrist, then climbed down the ladder, moved it to the other side of the crossbeam, and with a metal rod forked at the end, removed the spikes from Jesus's other wrist. Jesus's arms both went limp and fell against his side. The guard held his arm around his torso, which bent as if his bones had dissolved inside him. The youthful guard fought to keep Jesus's body from slipping from his hands, and it appeared to take all his strength to keep him from falling. I quickly climbed partly up the ladder to help him.

The three of us now guided the body down from the guard's grasp. It was cold, slippery, and so heavy that we all strained to keep our balance as Jesus's body was carefully lowered to the ground. For a moment, I stood looking at him as though I had simply been relieved of a burden I did not want to carry. Then Mary rushed to him and cradled his head while softly repeating his name. Once again, I saw his mother's horrible grief at the loss of her son. I knew I could never just back away from this man.

A few people had stayed on the hill. They now turned and began their trek down the slippery hill, talking loudly as they went. "What did that accomplish?" I heard one person ask his friend.

The other replied, "That man is harmless. Why were we so enraged by him? Barabbas I understand. A killer. But this man?"

Another chimed in, "I heard him once speak about another kingdom of peace and justice. Some justice for him! For that we had him killed?" I watched them and others disappear down the hill, lost in the rain, the wind whipping their words back and forth between them.

Only the women who had comforted Mary, the two other men, and I remained on the hill, along with the lone Roman guard. Someone asked about the bodies of the other men crucified on either side of Jesus.

"Tomorrow morning," the centurion told us, "the empire will send some others to remove the bodies. Nothing for us to do."

Shivering now, for the sky had begun to clear and the first stars of the evening began to shine in the blackened sky, we started away from the hill. The wind died down. Soaked, my clothing reminded me of how recently the storm had passed over us. It was as if the rain wanted to wash away all memory of the suffering, pain, cruelty, and grief that had gathered there in these last hours.

As we carried Jesus's body, we followed the finely dressed man I heard Mary call Joseph of Arimathaea, a member of the Sanhedrin. Little talk was heard. I understood from listening to Mary that Joseph had been given permission by Pilate to bury Jesus. Pilate wanted it all over—Jesus crucified, dead, and buried. No trouble. No controversy. No excuses in Jerusalem for an uprising.

Joseph and Mary were walking just behind me. I couldn't help but overhear their conversation. Joseph explained to Mary that when Pilate sentenced Jesus, he had started to release other prisoners, especially the ones held in the Cyrenean synagogue.

I suddenly stopped. I couldn't believe what I had heard. It couldn't be possible. I couldn't take it in. I quickly turned and faced Joseph. "What did you say?" I asked, surprising both him and Mary. "I mean, what did you say about the prisoners?"

"Why do you ask?" Joseph said to me, making it sound as if his conversation with Mary was none of my business.

"I have a son named Alexander. He was taken away from us in Cyrene. He could be a prisoner here. Maybe he was held in the Cyrenean synagogue. Is that possible?" I asked in a pleading voice.

"It's possible," said Joseph. "Pilate took prisoners for all the synagogues. He held them on the condition that the synagogues would cause no trouble at the feast. Now he's started to let some go, a few at a time. He feared the Cyrenean synagogue the most. Many radicals there. I was there when he gave the order to release some prisoners."

"Do you know the prisoners?" I asked.

"No, I don't. There're a lot of them being held. You say he's Alexander of Cyrene?"

"Yes," I replied. "I'm his father, Simon of Cyrene."

"He carried the cross for Jesus," Mary interjected, speaking to Joseph. "Simon didn't let my son down. If you can, Joseph, I'd be grateful if you would help him."

"When we've buried Jesus, I'll see what I can do. I have influence with Pilate."

"How will I know?" I hurriedly asked, my heart beginning to race.

"Go to the well in the center of the city tonight. Wait until it's dark. If I get him released, I'll send him there. If not, I'll send news."

Suddenly, my tears welled up. Mary moved quickly to place her hand on my shoulder as we continued to walk. Nothing more was said. I thought of how the death of Pricilla had left me feeling so alone. Now a deep longing for my son Alexander welled up in me once again.

I was glad that we were finally burying Jesus. I wanted to rid myself of the whole sordid memory of what I had seen and heard. The world I had once known now seemed strangely alien, leaving me with a strange uncertainty about my life. Could it be possible that I would see Alexander again? Even tonight? At the main well in the city? I couldn't let my hopes run so far ahead of me. Jesus was not yet buried, yet could

I really trust that this Joseph of Arimathaea had that much influence that he might find my son, much less get him released?

I feared another dream might shatter at my feet. The death of a man who was accused of insurrection, when he wished only to talk in stories to those who would listen to him—about another life, another kingdom, a better existence, free of sorrow, full of grace—had entered my life and altered what I thought I knew of it. Grief and anger over the loss of someone I had planned to grow old with had started me on this journey. Now I was walking alongside the unbearable grief of a mother for her only son. Grief for my own son mingled with hers. I listened to her break into muffled sobbing as we walked. Her son had seemed so innocent and so undeserving of this cruel death. And what had Alexander done? Pricilla? Weren't they innocent as well?

Joseph said that the tomb was only a short distance away. The sight of a beautifully kept garden, more like a lush grotto, surprised us. Someone, probably on Joseph's orders, had lit several torches at its entrance. Its mouth gaped open into darkness, and a large rock in the shape of a wheel rested next to its face. The light from the flames danced on the trees surrounding the garden, and drops of water fell rhythmically from the trees. Each droplet made its own distinct sound when it fell to the earth.

As we continued walking, I looked around at the perfectly trimmed grass and beds of flowers and small trees that grew here, some olive, some cypress. Two poplars grew close to one another, with only space between them for a child to slip through. The ground was spongy and soft, giving beneath our feet. I heard Mary sigh deeply, as though relieved to be bringing her son to his place of rest. She thanked Joseph, and I saw him simply nod his head, saying, "It's the least I could do for you."

We took torches and used them to light our way into the dark open mouth of the tomb. Inside was a marble slab raised about two feet off the dirt floor. It was white, unsullied, and pure in its appearance. We set the body down on it. Another man, whom I think was called Nicodemus, had us unwrap the shroud around the body of Jesus, which was marked all over with purple and blue gashes. Then, because Nicodemus had brought a sack containing a mixture of myrrh and aloes for the anointing of Jesus's body, we each took a handful and spread it on his lifeless flesh, under it, and in the shroud, so that when we began to wrap it more tightly this time, the fine fragrances rose up from his body. It reminded me of when Rufus and our neighbors had sprinkled Pricilla's body with some of the same herbs not long ago.

Here I was again, leaning over and spreading the dry herbal scents over another, this time a stranger who had, in a matter of hours, become so intimate to my life. Grief and death, death and grief. Grief turned to rage. Sometimes my grief erupting in such anger that I wanted to kill, to kill someone in revenge. How could these terrible couples keep dancing wildly in front of me? Could they not be put to rest? And how was it that now I seemed to feel the peaceful presence of this Jesus of Nazareth, whom we were now laying to rest, hidden away from a violent world? Had I not added my own violence to the cruelty on that march to the cross?

I shuddered at the thought, unable to escape the implications of what I had done with my own grief and vulnerability. Yet I saw what Jesus had done. I saw that he had accepted his own suffering without once striking back. Even in his feeling of utter abandonment, he had still called out to his Heavenly Father, questioning the heavens above from the depths of feeling forsaken. There was no pretense in this man, no elevating of himself beyond any one of us.

We performed our duties quietly, in silence, except for an instruction here or there. Sad but no longer weeping, Mary and the women surrounding her took charge. With our help, they turned the body so that the shroud was tightly wound, covering it completely. Jesus's body began to lose its shape as the cloth thickened around him. We stood looking at his shrouded body now hiding from us some of the brutality so cruelly inflicted on him only a short while ago. One by one, Mary being the last, we slowly walked away from an unearthly stillness.

As we emerged from the tomb with our torches after settling the body into its final resting position, I looked up at the night sky. It was clear and full of white chips of brilliant white light. They flickered back at us in what seemed like a harmonious rhythm. A horned moon shone. It would begin to form into a perfect white sphere in the following nights.

We briefly said good-bye to one another. Jesus's mother walked to each of us and silently embraced us. When she held me, she gently brushed her hand across my forehead and kissed me lightly on both cheeks.

Joseph's final words to me sent a surge of hope coursing through my body: "Remember, Simon of Cyrene, go to the well tonight. Wait for your son. At least wait for news. I'll do what I can."

"Thank you, Joseph," I blurted out. "I'll be there. I promise you. You know I'll be there."

XXVI

Exhausted, I went back to Rufus's home, where he and his wife, Yiska, and Alexander's wife, Nava, eagerly awaited me. All three were concerned about where I had been all day. They told me how tired I looked, and Rufus noticed the bloodstains on my robe.

"Father, what happened?" Rufus asked.

"Nothing," I lied. "I spent the day with my friend Zebedee. I helped him out. I cut myself helping repair his roof. It's nothing much. I'm just tired."

Rufus gave me a puzzled look but said no more. I quickly changed the subject. "Any news about Alexander?" I asked, turning the barrage of questions back on him, eager to hear news about my son. I didn't want to say anything about Joseph's promise of news for me at the well that very night. No sense getting Nava's hopes up. And I didn't want Rufus to go with me, in case any trouble arose.

"I've heard little, Father," Rufus replied, "except that Pilate is holding prisoners to quell any possible rebellion during Passover. I'm trying to find out if Alexander is one of them. He could be held as a ransom until Pilate knows the Cyrenean synagogue is quiet during Passover."

"Good, my son," I said. "Keep trying to find out what you can. I want to rest now." I started toward my room.

Yiska came over to me. "Before you go, did you hear anything in the streets? Did you hear about Jesus of Nazareth? They crucified him. So many had placed their hopes on him."

"Yes, Yiska," I replied. "I heard people talking. No one understands why he was condemned to die. I myself do not know. Please, Yiska, I'm tired. I'll talk more tomorrow."

Looking a bit hurt, she nodded her head and looked at Rufus. Out of the corner of my eye, I saw Rufus raise his eyebrows as though my behavior seemed unusual to him as well. I walked to my room, lay down on my soft pallet, and fell asleep instantly. I dreamed that Jesus had stepped out of an early morning sun, and the rays of the sun scattered his image into the shadows of Jerusalem. I awakened with a start.

I had slept only a short time, and I abruptly sat up. It was already dark. Far from a sunny morning. I quickly left the house through Rufus's shop, going out the back door. I ran partway to the well in the center of the city. I was irritated with myself that I had tried to sleep at all. What if someone had already come to the well with news about Alexander, and I wasn't there? I should have known I would fall asleep. I could do nothing but get to the well and wait.

When I got there, I realized it was still early in the evening. Alexander was not there. Drawing well from the water, a few women were talking with one another. Some men stood by, waiting to help them carry water back to their homes. How many times had Pricilla and I, and later our sons, done this at our own well? Several other groups of men and women clustered back from the well, talking softly as the darkness began to fall more rapidly, blurring the outlines of their faces. I eagerly scanned all the people. No one stepped forward to talk to me. My shoulders slumped forward. I began to resign myself to the idea that Joseph could do little for me and for my son Alexander.

Hearing splashes of water as the women lowered and raised their buckets, I thought of us all—Pricilla, Rufus, Alexander, and myself—at the well that morning when the four soldiers, Abenadar and Albus and the other two, rode recklessly into our family to change us forever.

I went to the edge of the well and looked down. Streams of water from underground fed this well as they did our well in Cyrene. So much had happened so quickly—yet not only to me. I was not alone in my horror and grief. I recalled what had happened to this Jesus of Nazareth, and the events of the day raced through my mind.

I looked more closely at the well. I saw deep grooves circling the top along its stone lip. Created over time from ropes lowered and raised, the stone had yielded to the persistent rubbing of rope in the worn grooves. How many through the years had brought the struggles of their lives to this well?

The grooves were deep along the inside of the well and shallower along the outside top. I ran my hands along the grooves. I felt all the efforts, the massive energy from the labors of mostly women pulling entire lakes of water from this well. The task never ended, for the water refreshed the inhabitants of the holy city of Jerusalem. Like the well's wounds, the grooves ground into the stone, ordering the lowering and raising of daily relief for those who thirsted. Could anything good come from those wounds so long in the making, carved into stone itself?

The well was comforting to stand by, to rest my arms on, and to look over its brim in the darkness ... to look into its black stillness. As time passed, fewer people came to the well. With each person approaching, my heart began to race. Yet no one spoke to me.

I took a small stone from the well's edge, where it had chipped, and dropped it into the water. All was silent for a moment. Then there was a hollow splash. I saw the stars reflected in its surface begin to shudder. The white spots deep in the water made me realize how much the heavens were right here, deep in the well's water. On some small scale, I had been part of both worlds when I'd grasped the cross and carried it farther than I had thought possible.

I leaned over the stone frame of the well and peered down. I saw my silhouette breaking up the stars' pattern overhead. I could not get over how the stars were in the water and in motion from the water's fading ripple from my stone. The heavens appeared in the water beneath me, deep in the earth, source of all life. Without this well, the town of Jerusalem would disappear.

As the stars calmed in the water and lost their motion, I saw there the image of Pricilla, looking up from the depths and growing ever clearer to me. She looked at me the way she did when I was coming in from the field after working all day to harvest the grains we needed to survive. I would stop and look at her. Often she would be waiting for me with a large pitcher of water from our well. I'd clean myself up before entering the house. The look she gave me told me she was proud of me and grateful for my labors. That is the look she wore now as she emerged from out of the darkness, proud of me in my labors. I saw her there and knew that just as the stars far out in the night sky were actually contained in the depths of this well's water, so was she part of both worlds.

Is this what Jesus had meant? I wondered, watching the image of her fade away now, deeper into the black water, her eyes intently on me and a smile growing so subtly across her face. Is this what he meant when he said that his kingdom was not of this world? Perhaps it was of another world, yet somehow present here, existing in a reflective way, right in front of us, to be seen in something as ordinary as a town's well. I was struck by the simplicity and the profound nature of it all. I found myself weeping along the side of the well. A few women at the well cast nervous glances my way. My tears dropped quietly deep into the well, mixing with the fresh water and causing the stars to shimmer a bit before they resumed their rightful form in the heavens.

A few more people looked over at me as they passed, but they did not come closer. Could it be that my tears had such power that they could actually move stars in the sky with their motion? My vulnerability thrown into the night sky? A few drops of water, falling into a well, moving the heavens with their particular power? Could one man, this Jesus of Nazareth, in his story and in his suffering, move the hearts of an entire people? Had he come here to move us into another kingdom of God here on Earth?

I had never thought about things in this way, content rather to move through life doing the right thing—some farming, sales to a few merchants, raising my sons, being a good husband. But with the death of Pricilla and loss of Alexander, and then this day of carrying his cross, something changed. Something shattered my way of thinking, like those stars in the well thrown into the night sky.

"My wife is not dead, really," I said to myself as I wept into the well. Or was it a voice telling me, "She is not dead but a part of another kingdom. And this other kingdom is right in front of you if only you were to look down into the depths of the water below, no farther than right before me."

"And paradise?" I wondered aloud. "Where is it? In the same place?" I remembered the words of Jesus to the young prisoner, who was so frightened, so terrified of what was happening to him. When the Nazarene told him that he would be with him that day, the words seemed to calm him, to take the pain away for a time. Words spoken to him, not me. Why compare my life to his? I had my own life to live.

I had lost my wife. My son was still missing. Joseph of Arimathaea had good intentions and yet no one had come to the well. I had been there now for at least a few hours, lost in my own musings. My reasonableness had been drowned in speculations.

The stones around the well felt hard and cold. I slumped down next to the well and leaned my back against the cold uneven stones, my head in my hands, wondering how I would go on. I heard a few people come and go from the well. Someone shuffled unusually close to where I was sitting. I took my hands away from my face, looked at two bare feet slipped into old worn sandals. I knew those feet. I knew those sandals, legs, knees, shoulders, neck. I knew the smiling face of my son Alexander!

"Father," Alexander said. "Father, let's go home."

XXVII

For two days, I basked—along with Nava, Yiska, Rufus, and all the children—in the joy of Alexander's return. He'd been released unexpectedly. Yes, he had been taken from Cyrene to be held as one among many hostages in the city to help prevent any rebellion. He spoke of Albus's remorse, and how he had come to the prison to beg Alexander's forgiveness. Albus had heard about Jesus. He told Alexander about him. No one had spoken of his mother's death on the journey back to Jerusalem. At times, Alexander wept with us as he spoke about his mother. He recounted the long ride back to Jerusalem and being held by Pilate, fearing that he would never be free again. Albus told him otherwise. Shocked, yet not surprised, he listened to me recount the brutal death of Jesus.

Alexander seemed most eager to know about Jesus, and he kept questioning me about the day I'd carried his cross. "Father," he asked, "what made him different? Wasn't he just another innocent victim?"

"I'm not sure," I honestly replied. "Victim is not quite who he was. He responded to everything that was happening to him. He allowed himself to be affected by all of us, even the children. Also, he seemed completely open to his Heavenly Father. So nothing human or divine escaped him. But he wasn't just taking it all. He was giving to us in the midst of what was happening to him. Responding, being affected, and giving back to us."

"I don't see why they killed him," interjected Nava, Alexander's wife. "What did he do to deserve this?"

Surprisingly, Rufus answered, "I think it had to do with the kingdom of God that he often spoke of in such mysterious ways, that it was like a lost sheep or coin or a grain of mustard seed … or a little child. This talk unnerved Pilate and even the priests."

"So who's to blame?" asked Yiska, Rufus's wife. "Are we Jews going to get blamed? Is it the Romans? Who's responsible for killing him?"

"Perhaps it's no particular group," said Nava. "Maybe he was condemned for enacting the kingdom of God. He put into practice what we've all been waiting for."

Silence followed as we pondered Nava's sudden insight. I couldn't help but think she was right. He couldn't easily be explained away. He had reached into something human in us all, putting before us a vision that required us to react in one way or the other.

I slept long and hard for the next nights. I found myself following Alexander around the house as though making sure he was really there. I would not lose him again. Rufus was clearly relieved to have his brother home, and Alexander's wife, Nava, could hardly contain her happiness. Alexander was home safe, safely home.

On the third day after I carried his cross, I awakened to a blue sky. With so many thoughts trailing through my mind, I wanted to leave the house and be by myself. I got up early, hearing roosters crow in the distance. I left before anyone else had stirred. The Passover festival had abated in Jerusalem. I meandered through the streets buying some figs, dates, and wheat bread for breakfast. Cleansed by the rain, the city had been washed and scrubbed. From a hill, I could see the shores of the Dead Sea. How I wanted to go there and sit, perhaps for a day or two, and think of nothing.

I walked past the Praetorium once more, again seeing the soldier in my mind reaching out to grab me to help the Nazarene and me, feeling inside a terror that defied comprehension. It was here that Alexander had been held, and I didn't know it. And now Alexander was with us again. How could Pricilla never know this joy I felt?

The streets at this hour were still empty. The rising sun cast its lights through the alleys of the city, creeping along the stones and illuminating them, as if a light were appearing from within the stones and shining out to light the city. A few torches still burned in the deep recesses of the streets. I made my way through the city's oldest parts. As I passed through the gates, they felt like an old friend. I saw the hill of Golgotha just ahead, and I felt a deep urgency to climb it, this time with a lighter load but heavier memories from my last journey.

I could see that all three crosses had been removed. My heart sank.

My first instinct was to simply skip climbing the hill and go around to the tomb. But something drew my legs up the "place of a skull," to the site of the crosses. Breathing heavily, I reached the top and stood for a moment to catch my breath. The earth still exposed the three holes, now filled with water, where the crosses had been anchored.

I walked over and stood before the middle one, wondering where the bodies of the two prisoners had been taken, since neither had friends or family present during his execution. It was a strange trinity of bodies that had hung together in the air for a short time: the one terrified youth drawn to Jesus's kindness in his suffering, the other recoiling from every soul that drew close to him. Yet Jesus seemed to draw them into a place larger than all the pain they had felt.

As I thought about their final fate, I looked down and saw that there were several small splinters of wood floating in the hole. I took up one of the bloodied splinters and put it gently to my lips. Salty tasting, it seemed to come alive. I slowly put the splintered pieces, including the one that I had just tasted, into a pocket sewn into my garment and stood up. I bowed to the invisible cross, and when I did, I felt the ache in my right shoulder once more. His cross would not easily be put down, I reminded myself. His way would never be an easy one, and yet I sensed that it could not be ended on a bloody cross. To this day, I do not know why I knew that. I knew there was more to it all. I had the distinct sense that nothing had triumphed over him, not even his painful death on the cross I had carried to this hill.

A surge of joy passed through me, and I wondered if I was not just confusing the joy of my son's release with some wild speculation about the death of Jesus on the cross. I only knew for sure that some deep joy was spilling over in me.

I turned and hastened down to the bottom of the hill as though drawn to Joseph's tomb. He had arranged for Alexander's release. He had done what he said he would, and I was filled with gratitude. Here, with him, we had placed the body of Jesus only a few days ago. Here in the early morning hours, the garden, with the sun drying the moisture on the plants, flowers, and trees, gave off a wonderfully unfamiliar aroma. Moist, cool air and the sun warming my face caused me to close my eyes for a moment to savor the intoxicating mixture of smells. I looked toward the sun and remembered my dream: Jesus cast forth on the rays of the sun, scattered far and wide, beginning with Jerusalem.

Pruning shrubs, two young people, a man and a woman in their early twenties, looked up at me and then continued their work, sweeping up leaves and debris that had fallen during the recent rains. The young woman gathered olives that lay strewn beneath four olive trees growing on either side of the tomb. I acknowledged them with a slight bow. They smiled but did not speak, concentrating instead on their work.

Reaching the tomb, I saw with alarm that the stone was rolled halfway back from the entrance, which loomed dark and very silent in the morning air. Suddenly, a woman emerged from within the tomb. She clearly recognized me, saying her name was Mary Magdalene. Then she immediately said, "You bore his cross."

"I did," I responded, now recognizing her as a woman who had held Jesus's mother at the foot of his cross.

"Mary has spoken fondly of you."

"Where is his body?" I asked, surprising myself with the urgency in my voice. "Has someone stolen it?"

"No," she said. "He is not here. He's gone before us." With these words, she took my hand and led me into the dark, silent space that we all thought to be Jesus's final resting place.

"Come with me," Mary said, peering into the darkness of the tomb. "I arrived here only a short time before you came to see him. I thought that after three days, the body needed to be anointed again with oils and spices to slow the decay. I came early to pray and to be with him alone. But look here."

My eyes grew accustomed to the darkness as streaks of sunlight entered the threshold of the tomb. On the marble slab where the body was placed a few days earlier lay the crumpled white linen sheet that had been the wrapping for his body. Pieces of the herbs and spices, still wet and clumped in small clusters, fell to the ground as Mary gathered them into her hands. "I can smell his body in this," she said, lifting the sheet to her nose. "I have to find Simon Peter and the others. They need to know."

"Need to know what?"

"That he's gone. He's not here. I've got to go."

"Mary," I said, reaching into my pocket and drawing from it one of the splinters of damp wood. I handed it to her. "This is what is left of the cross. I gathered a few pieces of wood this morning." She took it in her hand and stared at it in the darkness. Then she closed her fist over it. I saw that instead of putting it away, she carried it in her fist.

"Thank you for this," she said, and then she left. I sat there by myself, in the darkness of the tomb, as the light from the east found its way across the floor and crept slowly toward my sandals. Jesus's presence still filled the small enclosure. I did not want to leave him, even though he was nowhere to be found. At least not here.

I saw the two gardeners outside and thought to ask them if they had seen anyone around when they came to clean up the site. I approached the young woman and asked, "Has anyone taken the body from the tomb? Was the stone already pushed back by the time you arrived this morning?"

She suddenly stopped sweeping and replied, "Why look among the dead for the living? He is not here."

"But where is he?" I asked, mystified by her response.

She seemed to look through and yet beyond me, and without hesitation, she simply said, "The glory of God in the face of Jesus Christ is now appearing everywhere! The kingdom of God has begun among us."

I was astonished at her response. I stepped back in amazement. What was she saying? Is this what Nava meant? Jesus had put into our world the present and yet future kingdom of God? Bewildered, I turned and walked quickly out of the garden. Did this gardener mean the same? I turned to look at her once more. She had disappeared.

I hurried out of the garden and headed immediately toward the city's gates and for home. Where was Jesus? How would I ever find him? I was sure there must be some explanation. Jesus, the glory of God on Earth? His body wouldn't just disappear. I could only think that something more powerful than death had happened.

From that time on, Jesus himself began happening to many of us in ways none of us expected. In his death, he felt even more alive to us. The fear of death and the inevitable suffering in life began to loosen its grip on us. He made our vulnerability and that of others easier to bear. At the time, I did not realize how close I had been to the mystery of his power. In his utter vulnerability, he had come alive. He seemed closer to us than ever. I wanted tell Yiska, Nava, Rufus, and Alexander what had happened, although I didn't know what to say.

Rushing through the streets of Jerusalem, I just wanted to be with them. I wanted to find a home with them again. At the time, I didn't realize I was already home.

Epilogue

I've grown older now. The earth is pulling me down toward her. I have stayed and lived near my families in Jerusalem. I have lived long enough to see my grandchildren grow up and become mothers and fathers themselves. I no longer look so far off to the distant horizon but enjoy more fully what comes my way each day.

A number of people come to my home, where we remember for each other our experiences of Jesus of Nazareth. I've heard many stories about him through the years. Those who knew him well tried, often through stories, to explain the mystery of his presence among us. Mostly these stories were passed on to us by word of mouth, and those who told the stories, as has been the case for centuries among us Jews, were very careful about telling them accurately. As you know, in his gospel, Mark made a brief reference to my being compelled to carry the cross of Jesus.

As some of us aged, like the writer Mark and me, we thought it important, before we died, to write down some of what we had heard and understood about Jesus of Nazareth. Hence, I'm leaving this fuller account, along with Mark's and those of some others as well. Mine is more detailed than some of the other records. I hope it will not be lost.

It turns out that quite a few people, immediately after his death, also felt Jesus's living presence. Some even claimed to have seen him appear in Galilee and other places as well. In spite of our fear and sadness that he was killed, Jesus seemed to be saying he was not done with us at all. He would not leave us alone, ever. He would be with us in another way when we gathered and celebrated a meal. He had become a new Passover for us—new and yet deeply connected to all that we had been in our own life as Jews in Jerusalem.

It's hard to say how these celebrations arose around the city and surrounding area. There are many now. We continue life together in his presence when we meet in my home and in other places around the city. Rufus and Alexander, their wives, and now their grown children with young children, regularly come for our celebrations. My grandson Justin has become a follower of the Nazarene and a leader as well. He often leads a celebration in his home. I heard that James, who helped me for a few moments when I carried Jesus's cross, has become an important leader of a group of followers in Rome. It's as though we've all become the extended family of the crucified Jesus of Nazareth.

We've taken the language and stories at hand to best describe what we saw happen among us, as, for example, when some of us understood him to be a new Moses who came to deliver us and heal us from bondage. No matter how hard we tried to grasp who he was, Jesus seemed to elude our words and descriptions. In celebrating his mystery during our meals together, we got beyond our words and entered into life in and with him.

I never know who might come to our gatherings. Although many who attend are familiar, many are also strangers, although as we gather around a simple wooden cross we have made as a reminder of that day, there really are no strangers. People of all ages are there. Some, like me, are older. Others are children. Some are poor, and others have a lot. Some come with rather sordid pasts, and as I've written, my own life is hardly unblemished.

I shudder at the thought of how, out of my grief, I desired to kill Albus. Pricilla never would have wanted that. I would have died as a result. What would that have done to my sons and their children? I have since learned to trust in God's forgiveness for myself—a forgiveness that I saw in the face of Jesus that day on Golgotha. How else could I bear my past regrets and not cripple my future? I know God doesn't want that for me.

However, from time to time, I again think about Abenadar, and my anger suddenly flares up. Thoughts of Pricilla's last moments haunt my life. I've even entertained the idea of seeking Abenadar out and doing him harm. Yet when I gather with others, asking God's forgiveness and even speaking of my anger, I feel protected against my worst impulses … and even the lesser ones that arise on occasion. Called "people of the way," we have bound ourselves to him and to each other. In him, we see a new creation for ourselves and for our world, which includes forgiveness and new beginnings. A cross has been set in place between us and our worst, and even petty, intentions.

In those celebrations, we start our time together by walking in carrying a simple cross looking similar but much smaller than the one I once carried. It reminds me of the procession I took with him to Golgotha. We look up to the cross as we walk toward the table where we will eat together, acknowledging that he has changed our world in his suffering and death.

I have sometimes wondered if my own life is not simply a long processional—a long walk from Cyrene to the present. Jesus still seems to draw me forward into new life. I don't ever seem too old to become new in some small way each day.

Some people bring gifts other than bread or wine. We want to share what we have with each other, according to our needs. What we have is distributed to the poor and needy by a small group of people we've come to call "deacons." They go into the city after our celebrations, visiting the sick, those in prison, the poor, and the hungry. Some in need are having trouble with each other or just seem to be lost in life and have become lonely and forgotten by most others around them.

The kingdom of God is not here yet, and so we know it is our task to contribute whatever we are able, with God's help, to bring it about for both the present and the future. If, as Nava suggested, Jesus died to put God's kingdom among us, the least we can do is make our modest contributions to its creation.

When visiting these people, we bring them bread and wine, eat with them, and tell them the stories we've heard about the teachings of Jesus and what he did during his brief life among us. More often than not, this seems to alter their course a bit. Mostly they are grateful. As a result, but not as our goal, some join our gatherings, and our numbers continue to grow. I have heard that because of this, Rome is even more threatened by us, and some fear we are in danger of soon being persecuted for our allegiance to Jesus of Nazareth. As I said, it's all very mysterious. It's even more so for me as the years pass in days and moments. It's as though God's glory in the face of Jesus still dwells among us. It's so real.

Sometimes I'm asked, "Weren't you with him that day?"

Of course I answer, "Well, yes, I am Simon of Cyrene. But it is more like he was with me and still is."

I know I am not the man I used to be after I carried his cross through and beyond my own darkness. It was a cross I was required to carry. It chose me, and yet, as I leaned my body toward Golgotha, I unknowingly chose it for myself. Now I freely choose to carry it for Jesus of Nazareth as well.

Soon I will be compelled to cross over into a world that, because of this Nazarene, I don't think will be so strange. God's love has become familiar to me through this Jesus of Nazareth, whom we now call "the Christ." In time, I may know more fully what all this has meant. I may be surprised, of course. Who really knows? I know there are people who think this is all rather foolish. They have their reasons. My own reasoning fails me at times. Sometimes I simply have to act. I know enough to keep following him. I sense I've already partially entered a new realm. It's not at all unreasonable, and yet there's more at work here than I can simply explain.

I don't think you can bury the love Jesus showed us for very long. Nor will his kingdom be finally overcome by earthly powers such as Rome. The cross is now being taken up by too many of us, not that it's at all about numbers. God's kingdom in the power of the cross and in the life of Jesus is far too profound for all the usual understandings of power. The cross is just too much for empires and rulers, the powers of evil, disease, suffering, and even death. Foolishness for some, the cross, emptied of death and suffering by the love of God, has become new life for many, for myself, my family, and I believe Pricilla as well. And, well, yes, even for Albus and Abenadar. At least, that's how I've come to see it, in spite of all my doubts. So do quite a few others.

That's why when we leave each other, after we've gathered together in remembrance of him, we're in the habit of saying to one another, "May the grace, peace, and love of our Lord Jesus Christ be with you now and always."

May it be with you as well.

Photo by Hadley Asher

CHARLES ASHER, D. Min is a Jungian analyst, Episcopal priest of the Los Angeles Diocese, a former United Methodist minister, and an Oblate of the Benedictine Camaldolese Hermitage in Big Sur, California. He has previously served Methodist churches in Texas, Michigan, and Wisconsin. He is a RESEARCH PSYCHOANALYST under the Medical Board of California, and member of the San Diego Association of Jungian analysts. Along with his good friend and co-author, Dennis Slattery, he served as a core faculty of Pacifica Graduate Institute in Carpinteria, California. He also served for many years as the school's provost. He lectures, preaches, and offers workshops on Jungian psychology, dream work, and the relationship between Christian theology and Jungian psychology. He has published on contemplation, dream work, Jungian psychology, and the relationship between Jungian psychology and process theology. He has directed pastoral counseling centers, is licensed as a MARRIAGE FAMILY THERAPIST in California. He currently lives in the San Diego area, in Encinitas, California, with his wife and children where he continues to work on his tennis serve and the art of focusing on the next bounce of the ball.

E-mail: charles@drcharlesasher.com. Web site: www.drcharlesasher.com.

Photo by Pamela Sloane

DENNIS PATRICK SLATTERY, Ph.D., is currently core faculty member in the Mythological Studies Program at Pacifica Graduate Institute, Santa Barbara, California. He has taught for forty years at the elementary, secondary, undergraduate, and graduate levels. From 1984–87 he taught teachers the classics of literature in The Dallas Institute of Humanities and Culture's Summer Program for Teachers. He also taught for six years at The Fairhope Institute of Humanities and Culture's Summer Program for high school teachers under the direction of Larry Allums, current director of The Dallas Institute. In addition to dozens of essays on cultural themes and book reviews, he is the author or co-editor of sixteen books, among them: *The Idiot: Dostoevsky's Fantastic Prince* (1984); *The Wounded Body: Remembering the Markings of Flesh* (2000); *Depth Psychology: Meditations in the Field*, co-edited with Lionel Corbett (2001); *Psychology at the Threshold*, co-edited with Lionel Corbett (2002); *Grace in the Desert: Awakening to the Gifts of Monastic Life* (2004); *Harvesting Darkness: Essays on Literature, Myth, Film and Culture* (2006); *A Limbo of Shards: Essays on Memory, Myth and Metaphor*, (2007); *Varieties of Mythic Experience: Essays on Religion, Psyche and Culture*, co-edited with Glen Slater (2008); and *Reimagining Education: Essays on Reviving the Soul of Learning*, co-edited with Jennifer Leigh Selig (2009). He also collected and edited a series of essays on William Faulkner and modern critical theory *New Orleans Review* (1984). He has composed three volumes of poetry: *Casting the Shadows: Selected Poems* (2001); *Just Below the Water Line: Selected Poems* (2004); both with CDs, and *Twisted Sky: Selected Poems* (2007). He is currently co-authoring a fourth volume of poetry with Chris Paris (2010). Slattery is also revising a manuscript entitled *Day-to-Day Dante: Meditations on the* Divine Comedy *for Each Day of the Year,* due out in 2010. He offers workshops on Joseph Campbell and writing one's personal mythology to Jungian groups and organizations in the United States and Europe.

E-mail: dslattery@pacifica.edu.

LaVergne, TN USA
26 May 2010
184082LV00001BA/177/P

9 781450 202497